D3: THE MIGHTY DUCKS

D0063503

A novel by Jonathan Schmidt
Based on the motion picture from Walt Disney Pictures
Based on characters created by Steven Brill
Story by Kenneth Johnson and Jim Burnstein
Screenplay by Steven Brill and Jim Burnstein
Produced by Jordan Kerner and John Avnet
Directed by Robert Lieberman

SCHOLASTIC INC.
New York   Toronto   London   Auckland   Sydney

ISBN 0-590-05978-5

12 11 10 9 8 7 6 5 4 3 2 1   6 7 8 9/9 0 1/0

Printed in the U.S.A.   40

First Scholastic printing, November 1996

This book is set in 12-point Clarendon Light.

1

BRIIIIIIIINGGGGG!!!!!!!

Startled, Charlie Conway jackknifed up in his bed and blinked ferociously.

"What the? . . ."

He gazed around his room and groaned. It had all been a dream.

Just a stupid dream, he complained grumpily.

Charlie had dreamed about becoming a professional hockey player. It was *all* he dreamed about. He knew he had the talent. He also knew how to win. The Ducks had proved that by doing the impossible. They had gone from state chumps of the peewee league to state champs. And Charlie had been an important part of that championship season.

They had learned how to play as a team. But for Charlie the Ducks were even more than a team. They were like his family.

Charlie could hardly remember his own father, who hadn't bothered to spend much time at home. And the time he *was* home was pretty much forgettable. It was just Charlie and his mom, Casey.

Until Gordon Bombay showed up.

Charlie and Coach Bombay had first met when Charlie and his friends were playing on the District Five team in a peewee hockey league. Bombay was their new coach.

It had not been a glorious beginning.

The first day of practice Bombay cruised up in a black stretch limousine. Charlie and the kids had been suspicious. Suspicious but impressed. Bombay reacted to the kids as if they might be carrying some horrible disease.

Figures, Charlie remembered thinking. He was used to being treated like a loser. Charlie figured Bombay would be just like all the other jerks.

He was wrong. Bombay turned out to be the biggest jerk . . . by far.

As a hockey player Bombay had been a lock to make the pros. Then he blew out his knee—and his career blew up with it. He turned his back on hockey and never looked back. He became a hot-shot lawyer with a solid-gold Rolex and a platinum attitude to match. The guy was a shark in an Armani suit. He was all business. Shoot first—ask questions later.

Then one day his past caught up with him.

He got himself into a scrape with the law and was sentenced to do community service. His punishment? A thousand hours as peewee hockey coach to a bunch of misfits known as District Five.

It hadn't gone well. District Five was undoubtedly the worst hockey team of all time. They couldn't afford proper skates, equipment, or even uniforms. They couldn't pass, shoot, or play defense. One of them couldn't even skate. Not surprisingly, they hadn't won a game all year.

In fact, none of the kids could remember *ever* winning a game.

But that was a long time ago. And before Gordon Bombay taught them how to fly.

2

Charlie griped miserably as he slammed his fist down on the alarm clock. It was still dark outside. He fell back on his bed and stared up at the ceiling where he had pinned posters of some of his favorite NHL players. In the other room he could hear his mother putting out the breakfast dishes.

"C'mon, Charlie!" she called out. "Let's get moving. You don't want to be late for your first day."

"Says who?" grumbled Charlie as he pulled his blanket up over his face.

Today was the first day of the fall semester at the Eden Hall Academy, a prestigious private school in the suburbs. Charlie's mother worked as a waitress in a diner downtown, and the Eden Hall tuition alone was more than she earned all year.

But Charlie was going on a full scholarship. In fact, the entire Ducks team had earned scholarships. Hockey was big business in Minnesota, and it had been a long time since the Eden Hall Warriors had won a junior varsity championship banner. Figuring the best way to win a title was to get a team that knew what it took to win, the board of trustees had voted to award scholarships to the team.

His mother had been ecstatic. Going to such a "fine institution" was the "opportunity of a lifetime," she repeated to Charlie over and over.

Charlie already knew what he wanted to do with his life: play hockey.

The best day of his life was the day that his team had won the Minnesota State Peewee Ice Hockey Championship. He had felt like a winner that day—for the first time in his life. And it felt good.

The newspapers had dubbed the victory the Minnesota Miracle.

It *had* been a miracle. Charlie and his team had gone from losers to winners. They even changed their team name from District Five to the Mighty Ducks.

Bombay said that one of the reasons the Ducks had become winners was because they always flew together.

That was before Bombay decided to leave the flock.

That was before he decided to fly solo.

The day the announcement of the scholarships was made, all the parents and Eden Hall faculty and alumni were in attendance.

Bombay was there, too. But he had his own announcement to make.

"I'm not going to be your coach," he told Charlie. "I got the official word today."

Charlie was stunned. "You're joking. Right, Coach?" he asked.

Gordon shook his head. "No joke. The Junior Goodwill Committee has named me the director of player personnel. I'll be in charge of their junior hockey program worldwide."

"Don't go," pleaded Charlie.

"Charlie, I can't pass up this opportunity."

"But you can pass us up, right?" he shot back. "You dump us in some stupid school . . ."

Gordon took a deep breath and said calmly: "I'm not dumping you anywhere. Eden Hall is a great opportunity for you."

Charlie's eyes misted. "So you're doing me a big favor by walking out?" He scoffed bitterly. "My dad said the same thing."

"I'm not your father, Charlie. I'm me. And I'll always be here for you." Gordon smiled sincerely and threw an arm around Charlie's shoulder.

Charlie angrily shrugged it off. "Skip it. I've heard that lecture before."

Charlie walked away, feeling cheated. Eden Hall didn't seem like such a great opportunity now.

3

Inside the terminal of the Minneapolis airport a tall boy in blue jeans and cowboy boots strutted down the exit ramp into the reception area.

"Howdy, Minnesota!" he bellowed, greeting no one in particular. He whipped off his cowboy hat and waved it in the air. "It sure is great to be back!"

Just then a tram driven by a young woman in a business suit pulled up to the gate and beeped.

"You must be Dwayne," the young woman said good-naturedly.

Dwayne smiled and gallantly tipped his hat.

"Why, yes, ma'am," he drawled. He then gave the woman his most disarming grin. "But you can call me Cowboy. Pleased to meet you, ma'am." He reached out to shake her hand.

8

"Oh, please," she groaned. "That makes me sound old enough to be your mother. I'm Angela Delaney. I'm your faculty representative at Eden Hall Academy. I'm here to help you get settled." She kicked the tram into drive.

"Well then, *Cowboy*—what do you say we round up the rest of your friends?"

Dwayne tipped his hat. "It'd be a pleasure."

A boy with a backpack entered the lounge outside the Los Angeles gate wearing headphones. He bobbed his head to the music. An obviously irritated airline steward was hard on his heels.

"*Sir!*" the steward called out emphatically. "You may *not* keep the headset!"

The boy turned abruptly. He gave the steward a puzzled look, then removed the headphones.

"Listen here," the kid told the steward. "I paid four dollars for this licorice stick with Q-Tips, and all I got was the Kenny G. audio channel and a Michael J. Fox movie." His tone was swollen with indignation.

He dropped his hands onto his hips and said defiantly: "I'm keeping the headphones."

"But it was a rental," whined the steward.

The boy smiled smugly and leaned into the steward's face. "And I'm extending the rental period."

Just then the tram with Ms. Delaney and Dwayne pulled up at the gate. Immediately the boy broke into a huge grin.

"Cowboy! Howdy, pardner!" He pushed past the frustrated steward.

"But, *sir!*"

The boy turned. "Here," he said, as he flipped the steward the headphones. "I was just messin' with ya!"

Russ and Dwayne high-fived.

Two Ducks down.

Outside the Miami terminal a young couple was wrapped in a passionate embrace.

"Hoowee!" remarked Dwayne as the tram pulled up. "Would you look at that!"

Dwayne and Russ looked at one another and grinned. They both nodded and then shouted, "Luis!"

Luis expertly wriggled free of the girl's embrace and, at the railing outside the gate, gave her a sorrowful backward glance.

Russ shook his head admiringly as Luis climbed onto the tram. "Man, Luis, who was that?"

Luis sighed and blew her a final kiss. He looked at Russ. "A girl I met on the plane."

Not far away at another gate, a passenger was

nearly bent in half under the weight of a bag he had agreed to help carry for a young girl coming off the plane from Bangor, Maine.

"What do you have in here, weights?" he huffed.

"Yup." She took the bag and hoisted it over her shoulder as if it were a bag of feathers.

She spotted a tram approaching.

"Hey, Cat Lady!" Russ called out as the tram zipped up.

Julie Gaffney waved and dumped her bag into the back. CLANK! The tram pitched like a rowboat in rough seas.

"Just one more stray!" joked Dwayne as Angela Delaney steered the tram toward the terminal for arrivals from San Francisco. Julie elbowed Russ and pointed. Up ahead Ken Wu was at the refreshment stand. He had spotted them and was running toward them.

"Check this out," Julie said.

Russ grinned. "The Wu*meister*!"

Ken Wu charged through the crowd in the lounge like a skier through a slalom course. He gracefully vaulted the railing with an impressive scissor kick and came up alongside the tram. Then he leaped and twirled and nailed a perfect landing inside the tram.

"Judges?" he demanded.

They all pretended to be waiting expectantly for the judges to post his scores.

"A perfect 10!" announced Julie in a breathless tone. Russ and Dwayne pounded their feet and cheered.

"I guess you guys are pretty pumped, huh?" asked Angela.

As if on cue, they broke out into a chant. "Quack! Quack! Quack!"

On the morning of the first day of school, Charlie ran into Fulton in an alley behind the bus stop. He was taking slap shots. Charlie cautiously rounded the corner and held up one of the pucks.

"You ever think about shooting into the alley, not into the street?"

"Not really."

He slammed another puck, which went whistling into the street. Charlie shrugged out of his starchy school clothes and slipped on his old Ducks jersey. He pulled out a pair of Rollerblades from his backpack and hastily laced them on.

"I just found out Portman isn't coming," said Fulton irritably. "He's staying in Chicago. How uncool is that!?" He pulled the trigger on another slap shot. *THWACK!*

"Oh, man," Charlie said. "Are you kidding?"

"When he found out Bombay bailed, he bailed.

He said he didn't want to leave his family, either."

"What good is one Bash Brother?" asked Fulton. "What am I now? The Bashman? Nah."

"We'll think of something."

Fulton shook his head despondently. "No Bash Brothers, no Gordon, a school filled with preppy snots. Face it—this year is really going to suck."

A moment later, Gary Goldberg tiptoed into the alley on Rollerblades. He was holding his head and moaning.

"Don't shoot! Don't shoot!" he whimpered. He rubbed his head. "Man, that hurt!"

"Sorry, Goldberg," the two boys chanted in unison.

"No problem," Goldberg said. "I mean, life isn't hard enough already. Now I've got to worry about being nailed off the ice, too." He demanded indignantly: "Why am *I* always being shot at?"

Fulton pointed out the obvious. "You're a goalie, dude."

"C'mon on, guys," said Charlie as he gathered up his gear. "We don't want to keep the preppies waiting."

4

Out front of a downtown restaurant, Guy, Connie, and Averman stood on Rollerblades. Guy and Connie were arguing while Averman studied a map.

Goldberg, Charlie, and Fulton soon skated up the street, reciting the familiar Duck chant. They exchanged a round of high fives.

"All right, Ducks!" Charlie said, "Let's move out. We're picking up Banks on the way."

Connie objected. "Why do we have to skate to school the first day? I'll be all sweaty and gross."

Charlie was shocked. "Ducks fly together."

A few minutes later they skated up to Bank's house.

"C'mon, cake eater," Guy yelled. "Let's go to school."

The front door flew open and Adam Banks—wearing Rollerblades— skated down the walk and joined his friends on the sidewalk.

Guy whistled and hummed, "Ooh-la-la."

Banks was dressed in neatly pressed khaki pants, a crisply laundered button-down shirt and tie, and a blue pullover sweater. His hair was combed neatly. The part was so razor sharp it might have been etched into his skull with a laser beam.

The kids burst out laughing.

Averman skated up to Banks and peered closely at his tie. "That a clip-on?" he asked. He gave it a yank. Banks yelped. "Whoops. Sorry."

"Hey," Banks explained defensively as he straightened his tie. "I care about the way I look. What's wrong with that?"

"Nothing, Banksie," said Charlie as a conspiratorial grin creased his face. "In fact, let us help you."

Banks backpedaled, but it was too late. Charlie, Averman, and Goldberg converged on him like a wrecking crew, messing up his hair and yanking out his shirt.

"There," said Charlie as he stepped back to admire their handiwork.

"A preppy masterpiece," declared Averman.

"Banksie," observed Connie with mock innocence, "what did you comb your hair with? An eggbeater?"

"Very mature," he commented sourly.

"Ah, Banksie," pouted Charlie, "don't be mad at us." The other kids began making slobbery whimpering noises. Slowly Adam's frown began to crack. He couldn't help it. A smile emerged. Now they were all laughing and playfully pushing and shoving.

The kids knew it. *The Ducks were back!*

"I've devised the perfect shortcut," Averman said. "Follow me." He skated off into the lead and one by one the kids fell in line behind him. Except Banks. He stood with his arms folded across his chest. He waited. A short time later Averman skated back with the other Ducks sheepishly in tow.

Banks grinned. "Which way, Columbus?" he smart-mouthed.

Averman shrugged. "Just a minor course correction."

5

After the kids settled into their rooms they met downstairs. An assembly had been scheduled at the auditorium to introduce the freshman team to the Eden Hall students.

The campus reminded the kids more of an elite university than a high school. The enormous brick buildings were covered in ivy and capped with magnificent domes. The grass was so green it didn't even look real.

"Wow!" remarked Dwayne.

"We're not in Kansas anymore," whispered Russ.

And it wasn't only the grounds that appeared pampered and well groomed—so were the students.

Dwayne sniffed. "Smell that?" he asked. He rubbed his fingers together. "Money."

Russ looked around nervously. "I think this place is running very low on the brothers quotient."

"Tell me about it," quipped Ken Wu.

"I want to know who this new coach Orion is," Julie said. "My dad said if I didn't like him I could come right home."

Russ snorted. "That's nice. My dad said I'd better keep my scholarship or he'd whip my butt."

None of them would admit it, but each was feeling a bit intimidated.

It was that same old feeling.

They're all better than me.

They came upon a group of students marching in a small circle and carrying signs and chanting. One of the signs showed an Indian warrior with a red circle and a slash through it.

Another sign read: "Native Americans Are People, Not Warriors."

Dwayne read one of the signs aloud. "Warrior name unfair and demeaning."

One of the protesters walked up boldly to Dwayne.

"You can read," she remarked. She sounded surprised. It was like he was a caveman dumbly mouthing out the syllables. She shot him a challenging look. "Now will you do something about it?"

Dwayne was taken off balance. "Excuse me, miss?"

"You're either part of the solution or part of the problem."

"I guess we're part of the problem," Dwayne replied. The girl eyed him curiously, and he explained. "We're the new Warriors."

Luis seized the moment. He stepped forward and declared earnestly, "But I'm willing to change." He sidled up to her and peered deep into her eyes. "As a minority myself, I am deeply sensitive to your plight. Perhaps you and I could get together later and discuss your worldview."

He leaned his face close to hers and flashed a pearly smile.

She shook her head sadly, turned, and walked away.

Back on the streets, the Ducks were in full electroglide as they flew down the street in a whipsawing V-formation. Moving to the point, Averman adjusted his glasses and quickly consulted his map.

He motioned right as they all turned and swooped around a corner.

"Whoooooaaa!" screamed Averman. The level street suddenly plunged into a ferociously steep hill. It was like the ground had dropped out from under him.

One after another they flew down the steep incline, faster and faster.

Goldberg was last in line and he nearly fainted when he felt the plunge.

"I'M NOT A SKATER!" he wailed. Then he barreled out of control down the hill. He teetered on one leg and his arms flailed like a windmill. "I'M JUST A GOOOWHOAWHOALIEEEEE!!!!!"

All of a sudden Goldberg regained his balance. He breathed a sigh of relief—until he realized he was rolling down the hill backward.

Rolling faster . . . and faster.

"Uh-oh."

He flashed by one stunned skater in a blur, then another.

"EXCUSE ME," he called out. "PARDON ME. OUT OF MY WAY . . . GOALIE COMIN' THROUGH!"

The varsity "welcoming committee" was waiting to greet the freshman team as it entered the auditorium. The varsity players included Rick Riley, the handsome captain of the varsity hockey team, and Cole Sutherland, his burly, thick-necked sidekick. Cole was his enforcer—on and off the ice. The rest of the varsity team loitered at the back of the hall with the cheerleaders.

It was obvious from the look of smug superiority on the face of Rick Riley that he believed he ruled Eden Hall Academy.

With his arm draped over the shoulders of Mindy Pinkerton, the head cheerleader, Rick waited for just the right moment.

As the Ducks walked by, Rick stepped in front of Russ. Cole and the rest of the varsity team followed.

"You don't belong here," Rick hissed. "We don't need you ruining our good name."

"I'll give you a good name," said Russ pleasantly. "Otto."

Rick was momentarily confused. "Otto?" he repeated.

"Yeah," explained Russ as he pushed his face up into Rick's. "Like in *otto* my face before I knock you into the next grade."

Rick's face darkened with rage.

"Looks like we got ourselves a real tough homeboy," Cole told Rick.

Russ responded sharply. "I ain't your homeboy, punk."

"Easy, Russ," Dwayne said in a friendly, neighborly tone as he stepped between them. "These fellers must think we're someone else." Dwayne extended his hand to Rick. "I'm Dwayne. Nice to meet you. We're the new hockey team. And you are . . ."

Rick was seething. "The only hockey team. Varsity. State champs. My little brother lost his junior varsity slot when they brought you yo-yos in here."

Julie decided to make an observation. "He probably wasn't good enough." Her spunk brought a smile from Scott Vanderbildt, the varsity goalie. For a moment their eyes locked.

Luis, meanwhile, had been unable to take his

eyes off Mindy. She noticed him staring and gave him a sideways glance. Luis smiled, and Mindy quickly smiled back.

Rick was too caught up in the challenge at hand to notice.

"My dad," he said, motioning to the stage where Tom Riley sat conferring with Dean Buckley, "tried to keep you twerps out of Eden." He shook his head sadly and held his finger up in front of Russ's face. "He lost by one stinkin' vote."

Russ beamed. "No foolin'? Is that your dad up there? Nice outfit. Did it come with a yacht?"

"You want to go at it right now? C'mon," Cole threatened. "Where's the rest of you punks?"

"On their way, flathead. And when they get here . . . watch out." Russ coolly motioned for his Duck teammates to follow him, and they marched down the aisle to some empty seats and sat down. When they were out of earshot, Russ leaned over to Dwayne and whispered, "Where are those guys?"

Banks saw the road stop at a dead end and came to a screeching halt. When he turned around he saw Fulton thundering down the street toward him.

"WATCH OUT, FULTON!" Banks screamed. But it was too late. Fulton crashed into Banks at full speed. It was like being bodychecked by a Sherman tank.

Ooooomph!!!!!

The rest of the Ducks stopped suddenly, not sure where they were. Stretched in front of them were miles and miles of thick woods.

Banks turned to Averman. "Nice shortcut."

"Hey!" Averman said. "According to the map these trees shouldn't be here."

"C'mon you guys," Charlie said. "We don't want to be late our first day."

Dean Buckley approached the lectern and the crowd of students in the auditorium immediately fell silent.

"Welcome, students of Eden Hall Academy," Dean Buckley announced. "Since its inception in 1903, Eden Hall Academy has taken special pride in its illustrious tradition of excellence. Yet, as we approach the coming millennium, we dare not shrink from the specter of inevitable change."

Dwayne had nodded off in his seat. But at the mention of the word "specter" he jerked to attention. He leaned over to Russ. "What did he say?"

Russ shrugged, and whispered so that everyone could hear: "Something about a shrinking sphincter."

Ken and Julie burst out laughing.

Buckley glanced over at them. "Thus," he resumed, "the board, myself, and Tom Riley of the alumni association"—he turned to acknowledge Tom Riley sitting behind him—"have made a change for the future. So today, after much debate on both sides, we proudly open our doors via full scholarships to a truly gifted group of student athletes."

There was a polite ripple of applause from the students who were still awake. From the back of the room where the varsity sat came a smattering of boos.

"Oh no," groaned Russ. Buckley was about to make the introduction of the Ducks. Russ looked around the auditorium anxiously. "Where are those guys?" he asked Dwayne.

Dwayne shook his head. "I don't know. But they better get here soon. We're a few ducks short of a flock."

"Unfortunately," Buckley said, "their coach, Gordon Bombay—a former alumnus—will not be with us. But coaches don't score goals, do they?" he asked happily. "So please . . . "

Russ sank miserably in his seat. "Ohmanohman," he grumbled. Charlie and the rest of the Ducks were nowhere in sight.

" . . . join me in a big Warrior welcome to the 1991 Minnesota State Peewee Ice Hockey Champs . . ."

Behind the lectern Tom Riley sat scowling until his attention was diverted to a commotion offstage. It looked like a bunch of kids on Rollerblades.

". . . the gold medal winners of the Junior Goodwill Games . . . I present to you—"

"WHOOOOOAAAAA!"

Charlie and the Ducks spilled onto the stage as if they had been dumped out of the back of a truck. They tumbled, head over heels, cartwheeling across the stage in huge pileup. Averman and Goldberg collided head on—knocking Averman into the lap of an outraged Tom Riley, who fell backward off the stage. Meanwhile, Goldberg tried desperately to regain his balance by grabbing at a curtain.

He fell with a *THUD* and yanked the entire curtain down with him.

At last Charlie Conway crawled out from under the pile.

"Hi," he grinned sheepishly. "We're the Ducks."

7

The Ducks were told to report to Dean Buckley's office immediately after assembly.

Things were not getting off to a terrific start.

The Ducks waited inside the dean's posh office and gazed around the room admiringly. Then Charlie said suddenly, "Hey! check that out . . . Antsville!"

They all ran over to huddle around a giant aquarium in a far corner.

"Look at 'em go," said Fulton.

"You can learn a lot from ants," came a voice. They all looked up, startled. Dean Buckley strode across the room and stood for a moment in front of the aquarium.

"Brazilian fire ants," he said as if in answer to a question. "Even more important, they can teach you a lot about successful societal structure."

They all looked at one another with a *This guy is nuts* look.

"There is one queen and the rest are dedicated worker ants. Everyone pulls her weight. Nobody complains and there is harmony and growth. The same is true here at Eden Hall. You," he said, taking them all in with a sweeping gesture, "are the workers, the backbone."

"And you are the queen?" cracked Russ.

Dean Buckley took on a troubled expression. "Kids, I need your help. We've got a group of alumni and parents who are upset. They think that because they pay tuition their kids should get to play." He shook his head at the implied unfairness of the idea. "What we need is for you to keep up those grades and keep winning those games. Heck, I even expect you'll beat the varsity in the annual JV-varsity showdown."

Charlie took the bait. "Those rich boys? Shouldn't be a problem."

"That's the spirit!" Dean Buckley said. He clapped his hands and waved the Ducks out of his office. "Thanks for your cooperation, kids. Remember, we're all in this together."

Really? thought Charlie to himself outside on the front steps. *'Cause it sure doesn't feel that way so far.*

Charlie figured things couldn't get much worse. He was wrong. Things could get worse—and her name was Mrs. Madigan, the biology teacher.

Mrs. Madigan stood in front of the class with her back to the blackboard. In her hand she carried a pointer. She slapped it against the blackboard.

THWACK! Charlie jumped in his seat.

"EVERY MONDAY YOU WILL HAVE A PRACTICE QUIZ!" she barked. "EVERY WEDNESDAY YOU WILL HAVE A REAL QUIZ! EVERY FRIDAY YOU WILL HAVE AN EXAM!"

Her voice dropped to a cruel whisper: *"And every time I feel like it you will have a surprise quiz or exam."*

The class moaned. "SILENCE!" she roared. She gave the blackboard another *THWACK* with the pointer. "One more thing: there will be NO calculators NOR any moderen calculating devices allowed."

Russ shot his hand up. "Mrs. Madigan?" he inquired sweetly. "You made a point of stressing *modern* calculating devices. Does that mean I can use my abacus?" The class broke up in a riot of laughter.

Mrs. Madigan, however, was not amused.

"You," she snarled with an evil leer, leveling her dreadful pointer at Russ. "Outside. NOW!"

Compared to the nightmare of biology class, music was a dream.

It might have been the teacher, Angela Delaney. She didn't act superior. She acted like . . . a regular person.

"Let me know you're here and tell me if you play a musical instrument," she called out when they had all taken their seats. She glanced at her list. "Conway, Charlie?"

"Here," said Charlie. "I don't play a musical instrument. I play hockey."

"Thank you for your enthusiasm," she said. She read the next name on her list. "Dwayne Robertson?"

"That's *Duh*wayne."

She mouthed an apology and tried again. "Duhwayne."

Dwayne beamed. "Call me Cowboy."

Ms. Delaney put down her list. "Right. But Dwayne is such a beautiful name."

Dwayne blushed scarlet. "Aw, shucks, ma'am. It ain't as . . . *beautiful* . . . as all that."

"Sure it is," she said. "I used to hate my name, too. But some of the coolest cats ever have had some really strange names."

She rattled them off. "Wolfgang Amadeus Mozart. Igor Stravinsky. Thelonius Monk."

"And I'll tell you something else," she said. "You're going to meet all of them in here. And you're going to see their names are cool because *they* are cool." She paused and smiled. "Just like you."

No doubt about it. Angela Delaney *was* cool.

In the hallway Luis was leaning casually against a locker as he watched Mindy glide toward him.

"She's magnificent."

Ken Wu sighed. "She's also the head cheerleader," he reminded Luis. "And her boyfriend just happens to be captain of the varsity hockey team. And just a short time ago he and his goon promised to rearrange our faces with their fists."

Luis smiled dreamily. "I am in love, my friend."

"C'mon, Luis," pleaded Ken. "Snap out of it. If Rick sees you making eyes at his babe he's going to kill you."

At that moment, Rick and Cole turned a corner and stopped dead in their tracks. Rick did a slow burn when he saw Luis.

"Hey," said Cole. "Isn't that a freshman twerp making eyes at Mindy?"

Rick gnashed his teeth. "Let's get Chippy!"

They marched up the hallway and came up alongside Luis. "Hey there, Chippy!" Rick greeted him.

At the same time Cole lowered his brawny shoulder and checked him hard into the lockers. Luis grunted and crumpled to the floor.

"Oops," Cole said in mock concern. "Hope I didn't hurt . . . the little twerp." He and Rick laughed and high-fived. Then Cole grabbed Ken's lunch bag, whipped out an apple, and took a huge, slobbering bite.

"Enjoy your lunch," said Rick. Then they walked off.

Charlie turned a corner and bumped into Linda Chavez.

She spun around and held out a clipboard. "Hi! Will you sign a petition?"

Charlie was dazzled. He didn't know what to say. He stood there mutely, unable to speak. Linda Chavez was gorgeous.

"Hello in there," she said, waving her hand in

front of his face.

"Huh?" Charlie mumbled in a daze.

She laughed sweetly. "The petition?"

"Oh . . . yeah . . . sure," he said after an instant, taking off his backpack. "What's it for?"

"We're demanding that the board change the demeaning Warrior name. It's an insult to all Native Americans."

Charlie didn't understand. "Warriors isn't so bad, is it?" he asked. She eyed him skeptically.

"I mean," he explained hurriedly, "you got the Indians, the Braves, the Redskins . . ."

It was as if a light clicked on inside her head. She shook her head disappointedly and yanked the clipboard out of his hands.

"You're a jock, aren't you?"

Charlie puffed up with pride. "I play hockey," he beamed. "In fact, I'm captain—"

"Forget it," Linda Chavez snapped impatiently. "You Warrior jocks are all the same. You all stick together." Abruptly, she turned and walked off.

"I'm not a Warrior," Charlie answered defensively. "I'm a Duck!"

9

Coach Wilson had just blown his whistle, ending a typically bruising practice for the varsity hockey players. As they skated off the ice, the freshman team was heading up the ramp from the locker room for their first practice.

"So, where is this almighty Coach Orion?" asked Russ as the team waited on the bleachers.

"Who cares?" said Charlie impatiently. "This is our team. We'll win no matter who this guy is." A few of the players muttered in agreement. Charlie jumped up. "What do you say, Cowboy? Is it time for a roundup?"

This brought a knowing smile from Dwayne.

"YEEHAW!" whooped Dwayne as he whipped out a lasso. "ROUND 'EM UP, DOGIES!"

Dwayne singled out Charlie from the pack of

fleeing Ducks and bore down on him, swinging his rope. Charlie zigged. He zagged. He sneaked a peek over his shoulder just as Dwayne let his rope fly.

Caught! Dwayne jerked the rope tight and brought Charlie up short like a roped calf. He tumbled face forward onto the ice.

All Charlie could see were two extremely powerful legs pumping toward him down the ice. The skates slashed to a stop just inches from Charlie's face. Charlie peered up at the man with the whistle.

"My name is Coach Orion," he said, staring down at Charlie.

Charlie wiggled out of the rope and climbed to his feet. He smiled at Coach Orion. "Hi," Charlie said. "You can call me Charlie." The rest of the team skated over and huddled behind Charlie.

"That must be what the *C* on your jersey stands for," Coach Orion suggested. "It sure doesn't stand for captain."

"Sorry," Russ apologized. "We were just messin' around."

"Bombay gave him the *C*," Goldberg pointed out.

"I respect that," Orion answered. He added bluntly, "But that is the past. And I am the present. This is my team and I will select the captain."

Charlie was wounded. "You're kidding!" he lashed out unwisely. "You're the rookie here. We've been together for four years."

"Okay, Charlie," Coach Orion ordered. "Laps . . . now!"

Charlie glared at him defiantly. Orion calmly returned the stare. Finally, Charlie snapped.

"Fine," he said briskly. "How many, Coach Orion?"

"I don't recall saying, Charlie." Then Coach Orion gave Charlie a hard-as-nails, point-blank look. "Now GO!"

Charlie skated off angrily to the sidelines.

Coach Orion had sent them a message. And it didn't take a genius from Eden Hall to decode it: This was his team. Period.

Coach Orion began coiling the rope around his hand. "Now listen up," he ordered. "And listen good." They obediently snapped to attention and huddled up. "We are here for one reason. And one reason only. Do you know what that reason is? It starts with a *W*."

"To win, Coach Orion, sir!" suggested Averman.

"No!" Orion shot back. "To work! High school hockey is very hard work. And it all begins with DEFENSE." He paused.

"You're not kids or little ducks anymore," resumed the coach. "I won't treat you that way.

You're going to learn to play two-way hockey."
He explained what that meant. "Offense and
defense. But it's going to take one thing . . .
starts with a *W*."

Averman decided to take another crack at it.

"Work, Coach Orion, sir!"

"Wrong . . . WILL!"

"Sheeesh," muttered Averman to himself. O for
two.

"It's going to take real will if you want to play
in my barn." Coach Orion concluded. Things
were definitely going to be different.

10

There was at least one more important lesson the Ducks would learn from Coach Orion that afternoon. The guy apparently had never heard of the word *exhaustion.* After about thirty minutes of brutal conditioning drills, the team was dead tired.

And the worst part was they hadn't even scrimmaged. No sticks. No puck. No fun.

Coach Orion blasted his whistle and ordered Goldberg and Gaffney into the net for shooting drills.

Fulton grinned at Banks, as if to say, *Finally.*

The team lined up outside the blue line and took turns skating one-on-one against Goldberg. Banks was first. He skated straight at Goldberg and faked left. Goldberg lunged, and Adam zigged right and easily flicked the puck into the empty crease. Beat him clean.

"Beginner's luck!" shouted Goldberg.

Dwayne was next. He scored easily. Fulton, too.

Orion was shaking his head. He sighed and looked at his clipboard. "Ken Wu! C'mon. Let's see what you can do."

Ken Wu skated up to the line and gave a little bow. As he maneuvered the puck toward the goal, he suddenly leaped into the air in a graceful, twisting pirouette. He landed with a flourish and threw his hand into the air triumphantly. Goldberg was so surprised he didn't even notice that the puck had slid right through his legs.

Ken completed his move with an awesome spin move that reduced him to a blur.

The kids clapped appreciatively. A few pretended to hold up scorecards. "Very nice, Ken," drawled Averman in a refined tone. "A perfect 10!"

Coach Orion blew his whistle disgustedly. "Hey, Baryshnikov. Knock that off." He turned and gave Goldberg a befuddled look. "When was the last time you practiced?"

Goldberg explained. "We don't really practice *per se*. We either play or play around. You know, have fun."

Orion stared at him blankly. *"Fun?"* prompted Goldberg. "You know . . . the thing that makes you laugh, ha-ha.

"I'll shut up now," Goldberg muttered miserably when he realized Orion was not going to crack a smile.

Orion blew his whistle. "Gaffney! You're up!"

Julie Gaffney quickly took up position in the crease and the team lined up again. Adam Banks's slap shot was a low line drive from about fifteen yards out. Julie threw up her glove and easily snagged the puck.

Julie "the Cat" Gaffney was on her game. Shots came at her one after another, but nothing could get by her.

Even Orion seemed to be impressed.

Everyone but Goldberg. "I don't see what the big deal is," he pouted.

Charlie was exhausted. His thighs ached and his lungs ached. He wanted to be with the team more than anything, but there was no way he was going to let Orion know that.

Each time he made a lap he glowered at Orion.

The team was in the middle of a stick-handling drill. Orange cones had been set up on the ice. Adam Banks was the best skater on the team by far, and he had no trouble weaving through the cones. Dwayne and Ken looked good, too.

"Conway!" yelled Orion unexpectedly. "Through the cones! Let's see it!"

All right! Charlie thought. He was so excited to

be back with the Ducks that he forgot about Orion.

The team muttered some encouraging words as Charlie joined the line.

He broke off the line cleanly and neatly negotiated the first few cones. But at the fourth cone he caught a blade and found himself leaning steeply, out of control.

He crashed over the cone and sprawled onto the ice.

Coach Orion shook his head wearily. "This is why we drill, Conway."

"The heck with you," Charlie muttered under his breath.

"What did you say?" demanded Orion.

"I said I'm doing my best," lied Charlie.

Orion upbraided him sharply. "Is that what you call it? Because if it is, there's not much point in your sticking around."

Charlie was stunned. Hockey was about the only thing in his life that mattered to him. That made *him* matter. He bit down on his trembling lip.

"Why are you picking on me?" he asked peevishly.

"I'm not," answered Orion. "It only feels that way."

Charlie swallowed hard as he watched Orion skate away.

Goldberg collapsed on the locker-room floor. "Somebody get a shovel and bury me right here," he groaned.

They were exhausted. Drained. Demoralized. They sat around the locker room with their heads down and shoulders slumped, too tired to even complain.

The locker-room door flew open. It was Coach Orion. They all jumped suddenly to attention.

Orion had an announcement to make.

"The Eden Hall Academy requires that you maintain a C average to compete. I believe that's a bad rule."

The team—surprised—reacted enthusiastically. And, as it turned out, a tad prematurely.

"I don't want any C players on my team," he said. He turned a sour face at the letter *C*.

"On my team you will be required to maintain a B grade-point average, or you'll be riding the pine pony. You have fifteen minutes after practice to clear this locker room. You have homework to do."

On his way out he pinned a roster to the bulletin board.

At the door he turned. "One more thing. Stay away from the varsity team until we play them in December. Is that clear?"

They all nodded as he exited.

"Fifteen minutes?" Russ said in disbelief as he sank groaning onto the bench. "Man, I can't move!"

Connie wandered over to the board. "Hey, he posted our positions."

Despite their exhaustion, they all jumped up and rushed to the bulletin board. There was a lot of confusion. The team roster had been completely rearranged!

"I don't believe it!" Fulton grumbled. "I play left side, not right."

"Third line," complained Russ bitterly. "That is major dis'."

The uproar continued as Adam turned away from the board. He was as pale as a ghost. "I'm not even listed!" he announced bleakly.

The players fell silent in outraged disbelief.

Adam Banks was the best player on the team.

He might even have been the best player in Minnesota!

Adam staggered to the bench and sat down. He looked as if he were going to cry.

"I'm not even listed," he repeated tonelessly.

"Yes you are," Connie said. "Adam Banks," she read from the sheet. "Third line center . . . " She looked at Adam wide-eyed. "Varsity?!"

Adam blinked uncomprehendingly. "I made varsity?" His shock was suddenly tinged with pride. "I made . . . varsity?"

A couple of players congratulated him. But Adam responded with mixed emotions. Playing varsity was a dream come true. But it meant an end to the Ducks. At least for him.

Resigned, Averman walked back to the bench and sat down next to Goldberg.

The goalie acted remarkably composed.

"You know what the great thing about goalie is?" he explained. "You always know where you stand. I just mind my own business and take my place between the pipes."

"News flash," said Averman. He put a friendly hand on Goldberg's shoulder. "You're riding the pine pony."

Goldberg jumped to his feet. "I'm backup?!" he demanded incredulously. Averman shrugged. Snorting like an angry bull, Goldberg charged over to the bulletin board. "How could he do this to me?" he moaned as he moped back to the bench.

"Hey?" asked Dwayne. "Who's Tibid?" They all looked at him curiously, and he pointed to the roster.

Guy walked over and took a closer look. "That says 'Captain T.B.D.' It means 'to be determined.'"

"Oh," said Dwayne. "I see." He hesitated. "No, I don't. That's your job, Charlie."

All eyes turned to their captain.

Charlie stood up. He noticed the black *C* stitched on his jersey. He swallowed hard, pulled off the jersey, and flung it across the room. Then he stormed out of the locker room.

12

When Charlie slipped in through the back door of Hans's Sports Shop, he was greeted by a familiar sound. Hans was standing at the worktable. Hockey skates were piled in a jumble at his feet. He was bent over a skate sharpener as he hummed along to a corny Norwegian record on his old 78-rpm record player.

The whirring of the grinder stopped momentarily. "School was not so good today, Charlie," Hans said matter-of-factly as he tested the sharpness of a skate blade with his thumb.

"How did you know?" asked Charlie.

Hans shrugged. "Only two people can open a door so sadly." He sneaked a peek at Charlie over his shoulder. "Gordon and you." He smiled.

"School's a nightmare," moaned Charlie. "Especially our hockey coach. Have you ever heard of Ted Orion?"

"Yes," Hans said, thinking. "He left the North Stars in his prime. I believe he was involved in a scandal. Gambling maybe. Or was it steroids?"

Charlie said, "We heard he killed a man. Either way, this guy is no Duck."

Hans looked at Charlie meaningfully. "Perhaps you can show him the way."

Charlie scoffed. "He doesn't exactly seem open to new learning experiences."

Hans paused, then asked, "The question is, are you?"

Charlie was taken aback. Hans was supposed to be his friend. Now he was telling Charlie that it was his fault?

"All I know is," he shot back peevishly, "things used to be great."

Hans nodded. "Let me show you something," he said as he picked up a framed photograph from the worktable. It was a picture of Charlie and Gordon and the rest of the team in their old District Five days. Charlie and Hans both smiled warmly.

"Man," Charlie remembered fondly, "that seems a long time ago."

"Like yesterday to me," said Hans.

Charlie looked away.

"He's gone," said Charlie sourly. "We're too small-time for him."

"People leave, Charlie. But they are still here." Hans tapped a finger lightly to his chest. "Here. In our hearts."

"Yeah, well, I'd rather see him still on our bench," Charlie griped good-naturedly.

"I know," Hans said as he slid an arm around Charlie's shoulder and slyly walked him over to the pile of skates. "Can we discuss this while we sharpen the rest of these skates?"

"We?" Charlie grinned.

Hans pretended to look shocked. "Okay," he admitted finally. "*You* finish sharpening the skates."

"No sweat," agreed Charlie. "You just have a seat. This should only take"—he noticed the enormous pile of skates and groaned—"a week or so."

"Good boy," said Hans as he he lowered himself onto his favorite old sofa and whistled with relief. In a few minutes he was fast asleep.

13

Goldberg and Averman were on the lunch line in the crowded cafeteria. Goldberg was trying to make a point. "So what if she's got a quick glove," he complained as he grabbed a slice of lemon meringue pie. "Who's got the better stick?"

"You do," repeated Averman tonelessly as he watched Goldberg load his tray.

"Darn right," said Goldberg. Meat loaf. Potatoes with extra gravy. Ham and cheese sandwich. Two Ho-Hos, three cartons of chocolate milk, Cool Ranch Doritos, pretzels.

Averman shook his head disgustedly. He felt sick just watching.

But Goldberg was oblivious. "Who's got the game experience?" he continued. "Me or the cat girl?"

Averman tried to reassure him. "You do, Goldberg. She's just faster and quicker. That counts on this level."

Goldberg had a sudden insight. "Do you think I'd be number one again if I lost a few pounds?"

Averman looked down at Goldberg's tray. "It might be easier to have her gain a few pounds."

Goldberg considered the idea. *All right!* he thought.

Charlie, Fulton, and Russ entered the cafeteria just in time to see Cole hassling Ken Wu. Cole was rifling through Ken's lunch while Ken was forced to stand by idly. Cole took a sandwich, crammed it into his mouth, then pretended to gag and spit it back onto his tray.

"Man," Fulton fumed. "I could maim that big goon. If Portman were here, we could cream all of them."

Charlie told his friend not to worry. He had a plan that would take care of Cole and his goons.

"They want lunch?" he said. "Let's give 'em lunch."

Julie Gaffney stared at the profferred Twinkies and smiled gratefully.

"No problem," said Goldberg humbly. "You're going to need a lot of energy to play on this level.

Carbo-loading, you know. These Twinkies are packed with energy."

"They are?" asked Julie.

"Oh yeah," Goldberg insisted emphatically. "From now on I'll be your nutritional adviser. No charge."

"Thanks, Goldberg."

A short time later Charlie reentered the cafeteria with Fulton and Russ. They marched nonchalantly past the varsity players' table.

"Not so fast, twerp!" barked Cole as he grabbed Charlie's bag lunch.

"Aww, come on," protested Charlie. He made a big play to retrieve the bag. "My mommie made me brownies."

"Nice fresh ones," added Fulton.

The varsity players erupted in mocking laughter.

"By the way," Rick called out to Fulton. "It's too bad about your Bash Brother. I guess he was scared to leave home."

Fulton bristled. "Portman isn't scared of nothing."

"Oohhh," the varsity players taunted. At the same time Cole reached into the bag and grabbed a handful of brownies.

"Hey!" he whined, staring at the the brown mess in his hands. "What kind of crap brownies are these?"

Charlie slapped his forehead in mock embarrassment.

"Oops!" he apologized. "I've got to ask Mom to stop using horse turds in the recipe."

Cole stared at the lump in his hand and went pale as a ghost.

"AHHHHHHHHHHHHHHHHHHHHHHHHH!"

Charlie, Fulton, and Russ grinned triumphantly as pandemonium erupted in the cafeteria. A stampede broke out after Cole flung the bag across the room. Generous dollops of horse poop plopped down on the tables like rain. Everyone was shouting and screaming and running for the exits.

Charlie pretended to dust off his hands. "Gentlemen," he declared, "I believe our work here is done."

"There's only one more thing we've go to do," said Russ.

"And what's that?" inquired Charlie calmly.

Russ and Fulton simultaneously pointed to the varsity table, and Charlie gulped.

"RUN!" they shouted.

14

If Charlie had any hopes that Orion might have morphed overnight from Nightmare Coach into Mr. Supportive Guy, he was sadly mistaken. The freshman team was skating warm-up laps and Orion was riding them hard.

"Work those legs!" he shouted at Julie. "Where's your energy?" Surprisingly, Julie was lagging behind the rest of the team—including Goldberg. She clutched her stomach and skated to the boards.

"I think I'm going to be sick," she moaned.

On the next lap Goldberg skated past Julie and commented innocently, "One Ho-Ho over the line, Cat Lady."

Meanwhile, Charlie was grumbling to Fulton about the grueling intensity of warm-ups. "This is total bull!" snapped Charlie. "I can't play for this drill sergeant."

"Play for us, the Ducks," Fulton reasoned with him. Charlie noticed that Fulton was struggling hard to keep up.

"Come on," Charlie told him kindly, slowing down to help him with his skating. "Bend your knees a little more. Let's go, smooth strokes." Fulton stumbled and Charlie caught him.

"Thanks," Fulton blurted, and Charlie nodded.

Orion whistled the team into a huddle, then noticed Julie by the boards still clutching her stomach. He called over. "Julie the Cat, what's the matter? Eat a fur ball?"

Goldberg erupted in laughter. "Good one, Coach. Fur ball, ha!" But Orion shot him a disapproving look.

"Just get in the net, Goldberg."

"Me?" asked Goldberg. "Sure thing, Coach." He looked toward the boards and grinned at Julie. "My pleasure."

Julie shook her head and groaned.

The team was in the middle of a "wonder drill." Five players—Fulton, Connie, Dwayne, Averman, and Russ—skated against two defenders, Charlie and Guy. The coach skated in their midst.

Charlie lunged at Dwayne in an attempt to intercept the puck. But Dwayne easily side-stepped him and Charlie twisted, sprawling onto the ice.

"I don't see a captain out there!" Orion snapped at Charlie. "Make him make the first move, Conway."

Charlie jumped up and hustled over to where Dwayne and Guy were jostling behind the net for control of the loose puck. He snagged the puck and skated left, but froze when he saw Connie and Russ charging him. He panicked and shot the puck across the goal crease, where Averman swooped in for the easy interception. He had an easy shot.

"Freeze!"

Orion shook his head disgustedly. "Where's the one place you never—I mean NEVER—want to clear the puck?" he roared at Charlie.

"It looked—"

"Answer the question, Charlie."

Charlie exploded. "I'm not a defenseman! I'm a scorer!"

Orion calmly scooped up the puck. "Follow me," he instructed Charlie as he led him over to the penalty box. "That's a misconduct. Ten minutes."

Orion held the door open and Charlie angrily sat down and slammed his stick onto the floor. Then Orion skated back onto center ice.

"Anybody share his opinion?" he inquired bluntly of the players. No one spoke up. The fact was, Orion had earned the respect of everyone except Charlie and Fulton.

After practice, Charlie bladed alone to the bus stop. He shook his head when he saw Linda Chavez sitting on the bench.

"Oh joy," he smirked as he plunked down next to her. "Is this seat taken?"

Linda Chavez looked up briefly. She hunched over without answering.

Charlie glared at her. "You're just like the rest of those snobs."

She spun around sharply. "I am not a snob."

"Right," Charlie scoffed. "You don't like me because I'm an athlete. That's a snob. You don't even know me."

"I'm sure if I knew you I wouldn't like you."

"Try me," he said. She eyed him curiously.

"Hi!" he began in a fake, dating-service voice. "I'm Charlie. I'm a 14-year-old, almost-six-foot-tall, nonsmoking Leo. Turn-ons include hockey, pizza, and music. Turnoffs . . ." Charlie pretended to think. "Oh yeah. I hate everything about this school and the preppy twerps who go here." Then Charlie blushed and added hastily, "Except you."

Linda laughed.

"Now you," he said.

Linda took a deep breath. "I'm Linda. I don't

like it here, either."

"What about pizza?" asked Charlie, pretending to tick off items on a list.

"I . . . like pizza," she admitted.

"Music?"

"Of course I like music." He nodded approvingly, and she smiled warmly. "I like Pantera."

Charlie slapped his forehead. "No way!" he said. "I love Pantera." He consulted his imaginary list again and chuckled. "So the only thing we don't agree on is hockey. What? Is it too violent? You don't understand the rules?"

Linda grinned sheepishly. "I have to admit that I've never really been to a game."

Charlie was incredulous. "You've never heard of the Mighty Ducks? They even named a professional team after us."

Linda grinned and shrugged. "Sorry."

"Really?" Charlie said. A plan was taking shape in his head. "Huh." It was now or never. "We have a game Friday. Maybe you should come, and after we could, you know, snag a Coke or something. What do you think?"

Linda considered. "I still don't know you that well."

"Did I tell you I'm allergic to nuts?" Charlie asked, then added in a rush, "Peanuts—any kind of nut—and I blow up." He blew out his cheeks to demonstrate. "I like REM, John Woo movies . . .

and I really like talking with you." He leaned back on the bench, exhausted. He looked at her. "What else?"

"I don't know. Just keep talking." Then they both laughed.

15

That Friday during the skate-around just before the first junior varsity game, Charlie spotted Linda in the stands. He smiled and waved. It made him feel good to see her there. He knew that Hans would be listening to the game on the radio back at the shop. But it wasn't the same as having him in the arena. And it wasn't the same wearing a Warriors jersey, either.

At the same time Dean Buckley was entertaining Tom Riley and several of the board members and distinguished alumni in the pavilion box high above the ice.

Tom Riley sidled up to the dean and clapped him on the back.

"Buckley, they better be awfully awfully good," Riley whispered to him harshly. "Otherwise . . .

they're out. And you, too." Their eyes locked, and the smile slid from Riley's face.

"Do we understand each other?" he asked Buckley through a big grin.

Dean Buckley nodded.

The players were in a huddle around Coach Orion.

"Think defense," he reminded them and tapped his forehead. Then he stuck out his hand. "All right! Let's do it."

"Quack!" said Charlie as the team slapped hands.

The players started, and Coach Orion glared at Charlie. "What is that? Knock it off." He tried again to kick-start their enthusiasm. " 'Go, team' on two!" he said rousingly. "One . . . two . . ."

They hesitated for a moment, then in a lackluster display of team unity blandly repeated, "Go, team."

Fulton skated up behind him and tapped him with his stick. He motioned with his head to the bench where Orion was giving last-minute instructions to Julie. "Let's show this guy what we can do."

All right! thought Charlie, as he and Fulton high-fived.

It was time to show Orion what it meant to be a Duck.

16

In the first period, the Warriors played like a team possessed. They outmuscled and outmaneuvered the smaller and slower Blake Barons.

The blowout that had begun in the first period turned into complete and total annihilation in the second period. The Eden Hall Warriors had piled up a lead over the Barons of 9 to 0.

From his perch in the pavilion box, Dean Buckley gazed out over the ice with a smile of serene triumph.

To the assembled alumni and board members he boasted gleefully, "I think we're witnessing the birth of a dynasty."

On the bench, the Warrior team cheered.

Russ twirled his arm and hooted. He looked up toward the pavilion box. "Whoooh, yeah! What do you think about that, Suckley. I mean, Dean Suckley."

Despite the lopsided score, Orion was pacing the box like a caged animal.

Fulton nudged Charlie. "Check out Orion. You'd think we were losing."

Charlie shrugged dismissively. "Who cares what he thinks? We can win without a coach."

The buzzer sounded for the third period and they hopped over the boards.

The period began in supreme confidence for the Warriors, but soon the Barons took control. After the Barons' fifth goal, the Warrior cheering section stood in stunned silence.

The Barons were playing balanced team-oriented hockey. The Warriors had completely lost their focus.

Charlie was furious.

He angrily jumped to his feet and smashed his stick across the boards. Immediately a referee blasted his whistle and waved Charlie off the ice for an unsportsmanlike conduct penalty.

From the bench Orion watched, expressionless.

Charlie continued to yell at the referee even after a few Warrior teammates skated over to calm him down. Charlie angrily shook them off. From the stands Linda Chavez looked down and shook her head.

Dwayne meets Linda and, as he reads her picket sign, realizes the Ducks are part of a Warrior controversy!

"Goalie comin' through!" Goldberg cries as he blades wildly out of control down a steep hill.

Dean Buckley applauds the Ducks' arrival at Eden Academy.

What an entrance! Charlie and the rest of the Ducks wipe out on the stage behind the dean.

Two varsity thugs, Rick and Cole, *explain* to Russ that the Ducks don't belong at Eden.

Mrs. Madigan, the biology teacher, barks her strict classroom rules at a row of openmouthed Ducks.

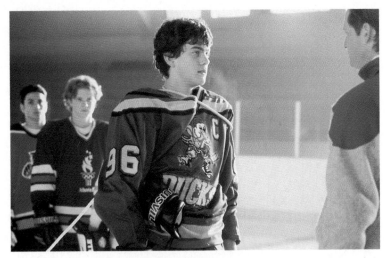

Coach Orion tells Charlie that the Ducks are *his* team now—and *he* will select the captain.

Upset by his confrontation with Coach Orion, Charlie turns to his old friend Hans for advice.

Coach Orion psyches up the team before their game against the Blake Freshmen Barons.

Taking up a post high in a tree, Julie and Luis direct the Ducks through enemy territory. The varsity players are about to get ants in their pants!

Just like a true cowboy, Dwayne tracks down Cole and ropes
him.

Gordon gently lays a Ducks jersey on Hans's casket.

The Ducks and the Eden Hall Varsity face off, this time on the ice.

A varsity player skates toward Goldberg with the puck, angling for a slap shot.

Goldberg times his drop perfectly. He smothers the speeding puck with his body before the varsity player can get a rebound.

Wearing their jerseys proudly, the Ducks pose for a group shot with Dean Buckley.

She had learned something else about Charlie Conway.

And she did not like what she saw.

Then the roof caved in on the Warriors. With time running out, the Blake Barons had clawed their way back from a nine-goal deficit. They hustled. They pressed. They bodychecked. They intercepted passes. They picked up three more quick goals and, with only 30 seconds left in regulation, trailed the Warriors by only one goal.

In the pavilion box, a grim and stricken Dean Buckley and the board members and alumni stared down at the ice cheerlessly.

Tom Riley leaned back in his chair. He wondered aloud, "Are you telling me my youngest boy isn't good enough for this team?"

Dean Buckley sighed.

Averman took Charlie aside to confirm strategy. "Clear the puck, Charlie. Kill the clock."

Charlie nodded.

The Warriors controlled the puck at the face-off. The seconds ticked off.

All Charlie had to do was protect the puck to preserve the win. Keep the blade to the ice and his body over the puck. But the empty Baron net stared at him tantalizingly. He wanted that fourth goal!

"No!" Averman yelled as Charlie charged up the ice. Charlie was at center ice with only one defender to beat when he executed his patented move—the Spinorama!

He could taste that fourth goal.

But this time the defenseman anticipated the move. He hipchecked Charlie. Instead of landing cleanly, Charlie caught a skate tip and sprawled, spinning on the ice. The Baron defender stole the puck. Suddenly they had the Warriors in a six-on-four power play.

Five seconds to play and the Blake Barons executed the power play to perfection. A slap shot from a forward on the right side bounced off Goldberg's pad, but a Baron center was perfectly positioned to tap the rebound under his outstretched glove.

SCORE!

The horn sounded.

17

In the locker room after the game, the freshman Warrior players sat on the benches with their heads lowered. Charlie sat by himself, brooding. He knew the team blamed him for the tie. But what had he done that was so wrong? he wondered.

"The guy tripped me in the Spinorama," he explained lamely.

"We didn't need any more goals," Ken snapped, glaring at Charlie accusingly.

Charlie stood up and addressed the team. "What are we even playing for?" he asked resentfully. "Some stupid school? The alumni?" He looked down at his jersey and scoffed. "The Warriors? I mean, what the hell are we?"

Russ jumped up and confronted Charlie. "We're on scholarship. And I'm staying."

"Fine," said Fulton angrily. "Sell out!"

Russ lost his temper and shoved Fulton. Fulton shoved him back. They began to tussle and suddenly they were all shouting and pointing fingers at one another.

A puck slammed—*BANG*—into an empty locker and everyone froze. It was Orion.

"How long does it take to score a goal?" he asked calmly. The players looked at one another uncertainly, then cringed when Orion hurled another puck across the room. *BANG!*

"Look!" Orion observed. "Less than a second. That means no lead is safe if you can't play defense. Get this straight! I don't care how many goals you score. I want one number on your mind—and one number only. Zero. As in shutout. Got it?"

They looked at one another. *Could we really have gotten off so easily?* their expressions suggested. They nodded.

Coach Orion paused on his way out. "Oh, by the way. Practice tomorrow . . . at 5 A.M." He smiled innocently. "You've got to get up early if you want to hunt goose eggs."

They all groaned.

Later, as they stood at their lockers before showering, Guy asked, "Hey, who took my clothes?"

"Me, too," said Averman. "Very funny."

"Uh-oh," said Guy.

They stared into their empty lockers in bewildered silence. In the shower room, however, they could hear the hissing of a shower at full blast. They trooped in and found their clothes piled in a single drenched heap on the floor.

The words "Freshmen Stink" were scrawled on the wall with shaving cream.

"This sucks," said Goldberg. And for the first time all day, they all agreed.

18

Outside the locker room, Charlie was standing in his wet clothes at a pay phone. He had promised to call Hans after the game.

"What happened, Charlie?" asked Hans. "It sounded like you just quit out there."

Charlie was in no mood for a lecture. "Whatever, Hans."

There was a pause on the line, then Hans asked, "Charlie, what is it?"

Charlie blurted, "I can't play this coach's system!" He felt himself losing it. "Listen, Hans, I'll talk to you later."

He hung up.

Linda had agreed to meet him after the game. She smiled when he walked up, then did a double take.

"I've heard of the wet look, but I think you may be taking it a bit too far."

Charlie tried to act upbeat. "Yeah. A stupid varsity prank." He apologized for the game. Then he pinned the blame on Orion. "Our coach has no idea what he's doing."

"And those refs were blind," Charlie concluded, shaking his head. "They definitely had it in for us."

"It was only my first game," Linda offered gently, "but I think you could have used a little defense out there."

Charlie pouted sullenly. "Great. One game and now you're an expert."

"No, I'm not," said Linda. "Relax, Charlie. It's only a game. Right?"

He spun on her and snapped angrily, "Right. And it doesn't matter if you win or lose. That's total bull."

Linda frowned disapprovingly. "Now you sound like a real jock."

"Maybe I am."

"I told you I don't like jocks." She turned and walked away.

Inside the freshman locker room several players were sitting on the bench, tediously blowing their clothes dry with hair dryers. The varsity game had just begun and the cheers that filtered through from the stands dampened their spirits further.

Goldberg held up a pair of sopping wet jeans. "I should have these dry in about two hours. Noooo problem."

"It could be worse," Ken said, and Goldberg looked at him doubtfully. "Really," Ken assured him. "Ever see what liquid nitrogen can do to your clothes?" All at once they looked at him, intrigued. "I spilled some in science class once. They've got this big tank in there."

Ken smiled devilishly and suddenly the mood in the locker room began to improve.

"How big a tank?" asked Russ pointedly.

"Not too big. Very portable."

"Sssssh," Russ warned Ken and Julie as they sneaked the nitrogen tank into the varsity locker room. "Okay," Russ whispered. "All clear."

They went one locker at a time. As a bonus, Connie and Goldberg squirted a generous dollop of shaving cream into every shoe.

The last locker they came to was Adam's.

"What about Banks?" asked Russ.

"He's one of them now, isn't he?" answered Julie.

Russ shook his head sadly, then turned the hose on the locker.

"Okay, let 'er rip!"

19

It wasn't too long before the varsity team charged into the locker room in a noisy victory celebration. They had crushed their opponents. Even better, they had shown the freshman team how a real hockey team played.

Rick delighted in predicting that Eden Hall Academy had probably heard the last from those jerks.

Then Cole flipped open his locker. His clothes were standing up by themselves. He reached for his pants . . . which shattered into a million particles of blue ice.

"What the? . . ."

He looked up and for the first time noticed the message on the wall: "VARSITY SUCKS ICE!"

Adam Banks took one look at his frozen clothes and sighed.

20

The next day in the cafeteria Rick and a group of varsity players stopped at the freshman table.

"Congrats on the game last night," he told Charlie.

"Yeah, right. We tied."

Rick shrugged. "A point is a point. Plus you made it through hazing." Charlie and Averman exchanged suspicious looks. "It's hands-off after your first game. It's Eden Hall tradition."

"It's true, guys," Adam said, reassuring them. "I asked."

"We're all Warriors now," explained Rick. "You guys proved you had guts. All set for dinner Friday?"

"Dinner?" asked Russ.

"It's an Eden Hall tradition. The varsity treats the freshmen to dinner. So round up your posse and meet us at six at Murray's Steak House downtown." He looked around the table, his face a portrait of sincerity. "Anybody need a ride, we can take you. You guys do like steak, don't you?"

"Yeah," Charlie said. "We do."

Cole grabbed Charlie by the shirt and lifted him out of his seat. "I don't like you punks, but this is tradition. And at Eden Hall I learned to care about tradition." Then he dropped Charlie back into his seat, and they walked away.

Adam was last to pass by. He smiled, and gave them an okay sign. "It's cool."

"Awesome lobster, huh, Charlie?"

Charlie had a huge mouthful of lobster and nodded. Rick laughed. "Hey," he told Charlie, "you have to show me that Spinorama move."

Charlie swallowed hard. "Sure. It's easier than it looks." He took another huge bite of lobster.

"No way," said Rick. "You're just being modest."

Farther down the table, Goldberg offered Julie a huge shank of prime rib. She elbowed him hard in the chest, and Goldberg tumbled backward out of his chair onto the floor.

"I'm just trying to help," he muttered as he climbed back up into his chair. Then he took a big bite of the prime rib.

There was a tinkling of glasses, and Rick stood

up to offer a toast.

"On behalf of the Eden Hall Varsity Warriors, state champion hockey team, I'd like to welcome the future state champs, the Eden Hall Freshmen."

"Hear! Hear!" the varsity chanted.

After the toast, Rick announced that there was one final surprise. Another part of the Eden Hall tradition, he explained. All the varsity players stood up and walked out as two waiters wheeled in an enormous cake, complete with sparklers.

The freshmen jumped up and excitedly crowded around the cake.

"The mother lode!" exclaimed Goldberg.

There was an inscription in red icing: "Thanks for the dinner, losers!"

Just then the head waiter glided up to the table and presented the check.

"Eight hundred fifty-seven bucks!" choked Averman.

"I think I'm going to be sick," said Goldberg.

"I've never washed so many dishes in my life," groaned Connie on the steps outside the restaurant later that night.

"We've got to respond," said Charlie. "We've got to do something."

Averman agreed. "It's like physics. Each action requires an equal—if not bigger—reaction." They looked at him, puzzled. Averman shrugged. "You know what I mean."

That night inside a varsity dorm room, Rick and Scott were snoring away peacefully as the junior varsity commandos set their plan in motion. Connie, Averman, and Fulton tiptoed down the hallway. At each room they ran a clear plastic tube under the door.

Outside, Luis and Julie performed surveillance. They were huddled high up in an oak tree that offered a perfect view of the varsity dorm. Luis peered through a pair of binoculars. Periodically he radioed instructions into a hand-held walkie-talkie to the tube runners inside.

"Little to the left," he said. "Good. Room B? Four feet straight ahead. How's it look to you, Cowboy?"

On the grounds outside the dorm, Cowboy sat astride a horse "borrowed" from the equestrian team. He surveyed the scene with a telescope.

"All secure," he barked into his walkie-talkie. "I'll go check the other side."

Meanwhile, inside the dean's office, Charlie, Goldberg, and Russ crept stealthily over to the aquarium with a large sack. They smeared a generous slab of honey inside the sack. They positioned the sack over the glass.

"Be careful," warned Charlie as they

watched a trail of hungry ants march single file into the sack. "They're not called fire ants for nothing."

"Are you sure he's not going to notice they're missing?" Russ asked nervously.

"I doubt he keeps a head count," said Goldberg.

In the parking lot outside the varsity dorm room, one of the cheerleaders climbed out of Cole's car, giggling mischievously.

"Shhh. I'm late for lights out," whispered Cole. "Just go home and I'll call you . . . whenever."

The cheerleader ran off. Cole jammed his hands in his pockets and walked across the lawn toward the varsity dorm. He grew suspicious at one point, however, and peered over his shoulder. He almost screamed. A horse was staring down at him.

"You a stray calf?" inquired Dwayne.

"What the? . . ."

Dwayne leaned forward on the pommel. "You know," he told Cole as he tipped his hat back, "it would be a heck of a lot more fun if you ran."

Cole finally clued into what was happening and broke into a run. "Hey, guys!" he shouted as he ran. "Wake up! It's a raid!"

Dwayne smiled broadly and scrunched down his hat. "YEEHAW!" he shouted as he galloped after Cole and flung out his rope. He lassoed

Cole. The boy struggled and stumbled and fell to the ground. Dwayne sprang off his horse and hog-tied him in seconds flat.

He waved his hat to the imaginary crowd.

In the hallway inside the varsity dorm Charlie was handing out final instructions. Connie looped a cord around each doorknob. Then she yanked the cord tight.

She gave Charlie the thumbs-up signal. Charlie nodded.

Outside Julie spoke into a walkie-talkie. "Release the hungry fellows." Luis couldn't help but admire Julie in her outfit. "You know you look good in black."

"Don't go there, Luis."

Luis shrugged and sighed.

The tube in Rick's room ran up under his sheets and up his leg. Outside in the hallway Fulton aligned the tube along the funneled lip of the sack. He grinned and nodded as he watched the hungry ants running along the tube.

The same procedure was repeated at each door.

Inside his room Rick stirred restlessly. He scratched. And scratched harder. He awakened, then threw back his sheets.

"AHHHHHH!"

All down the hall the freshmen could hear screaming and doors struggling to be yanked open.

"Easy, Connie," cautioned Charlie. He had his hand up as a signal. Connie stood at the top of the hall with a rope held taut in her hand.

"Easy . . ."

Finally Charlie brought down his hand. "NOW!" Connie yanked hard on the master rope. All the other ropes instantly fell away.

The doors all flew open simultaneously and the jocks tumbled backward into their rooms.

Finally the jocks escaped into the hallway, where the junior varsity was waiting dressed in full hockey gear.

"ARGHHHH!!!!" they shouted as they charged like a herd of stampeding bulls down the hallway. The jocks, hopping up and down, were too busy itching and scratching to protect themselves.

They tumbled like pins in a bowling alley.

"Oomph!" grunted one player as Goldberg checked him hard into the wall. It was a rout.

Suddenly Scott and Julie were face-to-face.

"Sorry about—"

Julie smiled sweetly. "From one goalie to another? *Save* it." She threw a look over her shoulder at Goldberg and shrugged. "Just a little goalie humor."

Rick managed to tackle Charlie. "You think you're funny," he snarled. "You think you're somebody. You're just white trash."

"Who are you calling white trash?" demanded Russ.

"We'll take you on anywhere," Charlie promised Rick. "Anytime."

"Tomorrow. Dawn." Then Rick ran screaming down the hall, scratching the whole way.

21

The next morning at dawn, the freshman team arrived at the rink wearing their old Duck jerseys. The varsity team trooped in a few minutes later.

"Hey," quipped Averman, "check out their polka-dot faces."

There was no exchange of pleasantries as the teams took the ice. This time around it was all business.

Goldberg was warming up in front of the goal when Julie skated over.

"We'll split the shifts. I want a piece of these guys," she said. Goldberg nodded okay.

Out on the ice, Adam skated up to Charlie. "They didn't tell me until it was too late. You've got to believe me."

"Right . . . preppy."

Rick and Charlie met at center ice.

"First to ten goals wins," Rick said, and Charlie agreed. "Full checks."

Charlie smiled broadly. "Oh . . . absolutely."

Rick easily controlled the opening face-off. He cracked Charlie with an elbow to the jaw.

Charlie winced and immediately tasted blood. He shook it off. There was no way he was going to let Rick know he had hurt him.

The pass went to Cole, who easily slipped by Fulton. He charged hard down the ice just as Connie and Guy converged on him. But Cole flipped the puck back to Rick.

Rick had the puck and an open shot. Score!

Moments later, Charlie led them in a flying V.

Inside the neutral zone, the varsity dropped into a defensive posture. They didn't appear to be intimidated by the Duck formation. At the center line, the varsity defender charged and faked a check. Charlie fell for it . . . literally.

The flock clumsily broke formation and tumbled onto Charlie. The varsity center picked up the loose puck and scored easily.

Julie slammed her glove onto the ice. "C'mon, defense! Let's go!"

Russ, Averman, and Guy hopped the board for the line change.

Russ was standing dumbfounded when Rick barreled over him. He was charging the net. Goldberg came out a few steps to cut down the angle. Cole swooped in from his blind side. Goldberg was an easy—and open—target.

Cole delivered a vicious cross-check that caught Goldberg under the chin and sent him sprawling. Rick came to a slashing stop in front of the net and tapped in the puck.

"QUACK, QUACK, QUACK!" he chanted mockingly.

On a breakaway, Connie shoveled a pass to Charlie. On the give-and-go he ducked a brutal check from Cole. The burly defender crashed hard into the boards.

Banks picked up Charlie and shadowed him as they entered the attacking zone. Charlie flicked a pass to Ken . . . and they scored!

After the play, Charlie skated up behind Adam and cracked him across the back. Banks slumped into the boards.

"Interference," said Adam as he jumped to his feet. "You'd be in the box."

"Go cry to your rich parents, cake eater."

"You're just PO'd because your precious coach bailed on you."

All his pent-up anger and frustration suddenly exploded. Charlie threw a punch that caught Adam on the jaw. Adam fought back. Suddenly both teams were crowded around them. Rick and Fulton started to fight. Then everyone paired off. It was pandemonium.

Suddenly Orion ran up and was screaming at them to break it up. He practically lifted Rick off the ground with one hand. "It's a damn good thing I'm not your coach. Now get your team out of here!"

They hustled off.

The freshman team hung back uncertainly.

"Congratulations. You have just forfeited whatever mental edge you might have had over the varsity. Now they know they own you.

"This isn't peewees. Your little Duck tricks won't work at this level. For the last time, stay away from the varsity. And I want those Duck jerseys off now!"

His order took a beat to register, but they began peeling off the jerseys and dumped them in a pile at Orion's feet. Everyone except Fulton and Charlie.

Charlie stood with his arms crossed defiantly.

"The Ducks are dead. You have two choices, Conway. You take off your jersey right now—or you don't play."

Charlie flushed red and looked to his friends for support.

"You're breaking up the best thing any of us had," Charlie said.

"It's time to grow up."

"Grow up! Like you? A washed-up pro who has to show off to a JV team? Gee, you're real tough."

Coach Orion refused to react. "Good-bye,

Conway. Anyone else?"

No one moved except Fulton, who stepped forward defiantly.

Coach Orion stood aside as he and Charlie skated off the ice—and off the team.

Coach Orion turned back to the team.

"No one is forcing any of you to be here. It's your lives. You decide what to make of them." The kids had mixed emotions. Watching two of their friends banished from the team was hard. But the coach was right. They had a choice.

Maybe it was time to put the past behind them.

No one said anything. But it was clear to Orion that each had made a choice.

"Okay," he barked. He was back to being a drill sergeant. "Twenty laps, then hit the showers." They broke huddle and hit their laps.

And this time nobody complained.

22

At a food court inside the Mall of America, Charlie and Fulton were munching their fourth hot-dog-on-a-stick.

A pile of empty wrappers and cartons were piled on the table in front of them.

"You want some more fries?" asked Charlie.

Fulton groaned and shook his head.

"Me, neither. Hey, you want to take another ride on the coaster?"

"Nah," decided Fulton. "Six times is enough for me." He clutched his stomach. "Anyway, one more loop and I might barf."

"Yeah," agreed Charlie. "Great, huh?"

Fulton smiled weakly.

Charlie leaned back in his seat and laced his fingers behind his head. "Sure beats school, huh?" Fulton didn't answer, and Charlie felt disappointed. "Tomorrow will be more fun," he promised.

Fulton leaned forward, thoughtfully. "Yeah, but . . . after that." He turned to look at Charlie. "I mean, we can't do this forever."

"I know," said Charlie. "I figure we'll go to public school for a while, then go play junior hockey in Canada. You only have to be seventeen to play."

"Charlie, I don't know if I can make juniors."

"Are you kidding? With your shot?"

It wasn't that. Fulton took a deep breath. This was hard to say. "I mean I don't know if I want to play hockey all my life."

Charlie darkened. "You're going back."

Fulton nodded. "We can deal. The Ducks are there."

Charlie felt betrayed. "Just go, then. It's all right." Fulton hesitated, and Charlie flew into a rage. "Just go! I told you I don't need you! Will you just get the hell out of here?"

Fulton stared at Charlie, then stood up and walked away.

Hans was sitting in his favorite chair listening to the Warrior game on the radio. A blanket was draped across his knees. When Charlie walked in he turned down the volume on the radio.

"Your Warriors are having a difficult time."

"They're not my Warriors," Charlie said glumly.

Hans nodded. "I see," he said as he pulled the blanket up higher. He coughed roughly, and Charlie looked at him, concerned.

"You okay, Hans?"

Hans waved off Charlie. "Is nothing. A cold." He motioned for Charlie to sit down. "Your mother has been calling, looking for you."

"I'm right here," said Charlie.

They listened to the game. The Warriors were down 4 to 1 in the third period to the Oak Crest Cardinals.

"It sounds like the team needs you."

"They don't need me," said Charlie bitterly. "They need a new coach."

"Coach Orion won't let you just skate by," explained Hans. "He demands more. He wants it because he knows it is there inside you." He put a hand on Charlie's knee. "Just like Gordon did. He needs you to lead."

Charlie looked at Hans appealingly. "How can I lead when he takes away my *C*, Hans? I was captain."

"It's just a letter, Charlie." He reached into a drawer and pulled out a handful of felt *C*s. "Here. Have one. I have hundreds."

"Don't make fun of me, Hans. It's not the same."

Hans tried to make Charlie understand. "He

took away the letter, Charlie. He did not take away what was underneath."

Charlie was confused. "What does that mean?"

"Under the *C* is you. Charlie Conway."

"Yeah, so?"

Hans leaned back, and sighed expansively. "So just be yourself, Charlie. Be the boy on the pond, loving the game, learning to fly. Be the boy who became a leader and held the Ducks together through thick and thin." He shooed him away with his hands. "Now go be with your friends. You are the heart of the team."

At last Charlie said, "I've got to walk. I'll see you later, Hans."

Hans watched him go. "Good-bye, Charlie."

Charlie walked for hours.

Casey had been waiting impatiently at the diner. At around eleven a bell jingled and Casey turned hopefully to the door. It was Charlie. Her shoulders slumped with relief.

He walked up to her.

Her hands shook and her face was streaked with tears.

"What is it?"

"Charlie," she said, taking his hand. "Hans is dead."

23

At the cemetery the morning of the funeral a large crowd had gathered. One by one the mourners silently filed up a shallow slope to a grassy rise. There—overlooking a meadow—the casket lay covered with flowers.

Charlie stood at the edge of the grave alone. His eyes clouded with tears. He remembered the last time he and Hans had talked. He had said things in anger. He had not had a chance to say good-bye.

And now it was too late.

Just before the ceremony was about to begin, a car approached along the winding drive, and out stepped Gordon Bombay. As he climbed the hill, heads turned in acknowledgment. He approached Charlie.

He spoke as if to himself. "When my dad died,

I felt like I was all alone . . . except for Hans. The great thing about Hans was that he was always there for you." He looked at Charlie meaningfully. "He was there for all of us." Charlie looked away. "Now Hans is gone, but we can still carry him here." Gordon tapped his heart.

There was a moment of silence.

"Every time you feel the ice," said Gordon, "just remember that it was Hans who helped us fly."

Charlie nodded, then walked away. He needed some time to think.

The next morning, the alarm banged Charlie awake. It was 6:00 A.M. Charlie sighed groggily.

"What? . . ."

Suddenly Charlie bolted upright. He stared at the clock, confused. "I didn't set the alarm."

"I know," a voice answered. "I did." Charlie whirled to find Gordon sitting at the foot of his bed.

Gordon grinned. "I thought we'd spend the day together. Get an early start."

"Go away." Charlie was sulking. "I'm staying in bed." As if to prove it, he slid back down and pulled the blanket up over his head.

"I know you've been going through a rough time," said Gordon sympathetically. "I can understand that. There hasn't been a day that's gone by that I haven't thought about you and the Ducks."

"There are no Ducks." Charlie briefly poked out his head. "Orion split us apart. You left us with a real jerk."

"Orion?" Gordon asked skeptically. He shook his head. "Maybe you don't know the whole story. Come on, get dressed."

"Get lost."

"Can't do that," said Gordon. He calmly lifted the mattress and Charlie tumbled onto the floor. "Come on, Charlie," he said. "Get dressed."

"Where are we going?" demanded Charlie in the car.

Gordon winked. "You'll see." After a short drive Gordon pulled into the parking lot at the Eden Hall arena. They entered the arena and Gordon guided Charlie up the stairs into the darkened stands.

"What's all this about?" asked Charlie grumpily.

Bombay pointed. A man in street clothes was pushing a young girl in a wheelchair around on the ice. It was Orion. The girl turned in her chair and looked up at him with adoring eyes. Both were laughing.

Charlie looked at Bombay, suddenly understanding.

"That's right, Charlie. It's his daughter. She

was injured in a car accident about five years ago. He was driving. They got sideswiped." He paused. "I've known Ted since peewees. When he quit the Stars he came to me to get out of his contract."

"So that's why he gave up playing pros?" asked Charlie.

"When the North Stars left, he stayed behind. He refused to disrupt her recovery. Her doctors and all her friends were here."

"We all thought he was just a bully who couldn't cut it."

"Oh, he could cut it, I assure you," said Gordon. "He just made a choice, Charlie. And I don't think he's ever regretted his decision for a minute."

Gordon and Charlie quietly left the arena.

"I just wanted you to see him for who he is," Gordon told Charlie in the hallway. "Sometimes we put on tough exteriors to hide the pain. I've done it a lot in my life."

They passed a trophy case and Gordon stopped.

"I was a classic overachiever. I was like you, Charlie, growing up without a father. I was angry half the time, and the other half, I felt completely lost and alone."

Charlie nodded.

"When I played hockey, I was a total hotshot. I

tried to take control of every game. I wound up quitting. So I tried law. But it's the same thing. I rule in the courtroom, but inside I'm a mess. Man, I was going down. But then this great thing happened. I got arrested."

Charlie shot him an incredulous look. But Gordon insisted.

"I got arrested and sentenced to do community service." He chuckled at the memory. "And as much as I fought it, there you were. You gave me a life, Charlie. You and the Ducks."

They walked on in silence. Then Gordon stopped and turned to Charlie.

"I told Orion all this when I talked to him about taking over. I told him you were the heart of the team." Gordon put his arm around Charlie's shoulder. "I told Orion you were the real Minnesota Miracle Man. So be that man, Charlie. Be that man."

24

The freshman Warriors were waiting in line to board the team bus. Orion was checking off players.

"Wu . . . Mendoza . . . Tyler." He hesitated. "Conway?"

"I want to be on the team, Coach." Orion stared back at Charlie. "I want to play two-way hockey." Charlie squared his shoulders. "Can I come back?"

"No," said Orion bluntly. Charlie was crushed.

"You can't come back," explained Orion, "because as far as I'm concerned you never left the team." Charlie looked up. Orion smiled. "Have a seat. We're running late."

Charlie hustled onto the bus, and Orion jumped on right after him.

"Okay," he instructed the driver. "Let's go. We got a game."

Charlie beamed as he walked down the aisle high-fiving his teammates.

"Oh, man," joked Russ as Charlie plunked down in a seat next to him. "Coach had you bad! You should have seen your face." He pulled a weepy face. "Oh, Coach, I want to come back."

The bus lurched forward. Suddenly it jerked to a stop. There was a furious pounding at the door. The door swung open and Dean Buckley appeared.

"Hey, hey! I almost missed you!" He beamed cheerfully at the players, then took Coach Orion aside. "Say, Coach, I wonder if I might have a few words with your boys?"

"And girls!" piped Julie.

"Yes, of course. And girls."

The team exchanged nervous glances as Buckley began to walk down the aisle.

"We have to think of the long term here. And believe me, this is very difficult for me. The fact is, I think you kids are a welcome breath of fresh air!

"Unfortunately the board doesn't quite see it as I do." He sighed audibly. "The fact is, they've decided to . . . well . . . to vote to approve the withdrawal of your scholarships."

The kids began to protest.

"Now, now," he said cheerfully over their grumblings. "You're welcome to stay through

95

the end of the semester. But after that it will be necessary for you to enjoy other educational opportunities." He concluded by clapping his hands together. "Now get out there and win that hockey game!"

The players slumped off the bus and then began to protest to their coach.

"We're just pawns," observed Averman philosophically. "Puppets in the big stage show, jesters for the king, barnacles on the underbelly of—"

"Shut up, Averman," snapped Luis. They were all thinking the same thing: *It's so unfair!*

"Is this even legal?" Luis asked. "I mean, don't we have contracts or something?"

Coach Orion shook his head doubtfully. But his eyes had gone steely and hard.

"We're going to fight this," he promised his team. "We're going to fight this hard." Encouraged by his determination, the kids broke into cheers.

"Well, Coach," said Charlie finally. "Maybe we should seek counsel." He grinned. "Know any good lawyers?"

25

The conference room was packed.

The twelve distinguished members of the Eden Hall Academy Board of Directors sat somberly on an oak dais at the front of the room. The freshman team, their parents, and a crowd of enthusiastic supporters sat to one side. On the other sat the varsity team and a large contingent of alumni, including a confident Tom Riley.

Coach Orion addressed the board from the podium.

"And so," he concluded, "I ask you to reconsider your decision to cancel the scholarships awarded to the freshman hockey team. I ask you to let them fulfill their four-year commitment to the Eden Hall Academy."

His appeal was greeted with a burst of

applause from the freshman Warrior supporters in the audience.

At the podium, Dean Buckley obediently turned to his fellow board members.

"Do I have a motion to reconsider?" he inquired unenthusiastically.

The board members sat in mute silence. Not one of them came forward.

Tom Riley smiled smugly.

Dean Buckley shrugged. "I'm sorry, Coach," he announced without the slightest hint of regret. "But without a motion from a board member and a second, the decision stands."

"I can't tell you how sorry I am to hear you say that, Dean Buckley," said Coach Orion. His tone was weirdly upbeat. He turned to look over his shoulder at Charlie, who smiled slyly and gave him a confident thumbs-up.

Coach Orion turned back to the board members. "You leave us no choice but to bring in our attorney," he concluded.

There was a confused fluttering from the board members at the head table. Dean Buckley clamped his hand over the microphone and began whispering frantically with the other board members.

The doors at the back of the room flew open. Gordon Bombay—dressed in his most formidable power suit—strode up the aisle carrying a briefcase.

Immediately the freshman team began chanting, "Quack! Quack!"

Bombay acknowledged the familiar greeting with a friendly wink to the crowd. Then he turned into pure steel. His tone was brisk and to the point.

"Ladies and gentlemen of the board," he began, "as counsel for Coach Orion and the freshman hockey team I am here tonight to set forth your legal options so that you might make the best possible decision for all parties concerned."

"Mr. Bombay," objected Dean Buckley, "must I remind you that this is not a legal proceeding?"

"Not yet it isn't," replied Gordon. "But I assure you that it will be." He flipped open his briefcase and retrieved a folder. "These scholarships," he argued as he held the folder, "became binding contracts upon the signatures of the recipients, to wit an acceptance by the Ducks. They cannot be voided except for cause—which, I guarantee you, you have none."

The board members were beginning to squirm uneasily.

"Should you pursue the cancellation of their scholarships," said Gordon to the board, "I will slap you with an injunction within twenty-four hours. I will tie this matter up in court for years, until long after these freshmen have gone off to college. And I will collect damages. I will win because I am very good. And do you know why I am so good? Because I had a good education. You gave it to me, and you will give it to these kids, whether you like it or not."

He summed up with a flourish. "Accordingly, I demand you reinstate their scholarships—for their benefit . . . as well as your own."

The Duck fans burst into wild applause. On the other side of the room Tom Riley and his alumni friends looked stunned. Dean Buckley and the rest of the board were huddled in animated conversation.

After a brief sidebar, the board members resumed their seats. The audience held its breath.

"I move the scholarships be reinstated," a board member declared finally.

Tom Riley was livid. He twisted angrily in his seat.

"I second the motion," declared another.

"All in favor?" inquired Dean Buckley.

One by one, all twelve board members raised their hands. It was unanimous.

A huge cheer went up and the crowd broke into a frenzied chorus of "Quack! Quack!" They had won. And it felt good.

26

Outside the conference room the players crowded around Gordon, exchanging high fives and patting him on the back.

Gordon turned to Charlie. "I've got some business in Chicago." Charlie nodded. "I'll be back soon. Call me if you need a lawyer . . . or a friend."

Charlie smiled. "Thanks, Coach." He and Charlie hugged warmly.

The team cheered again and Gordon waved, then walked away.

Linda came up to Charlie. "Hi," she said sweetly. "Congratulations."

Charlie looked at her. "Thanks," he said. There was a pause. "Listen," he said finally. "I'm sorry I was such a jerk. I'm staying in school and, well . . . ," his tone was hopeful. "I still owe you that Coke."

She took his hand. "I'm just glad you're back."

They were about to hug when Charlie was shoved hard in the shoulder.

"Congratulations," snarled Rick, "On destroying our school."

"It's our school, too," Ken Wu pointed out.

"It'll never be your school. Don't you get it?" Rick shook his head and scoffed. "Your fancy lawyer kept you here on a technicality, but you'll never belong."

"This Friday the varsity takes on the JV," said Rick coldly. "We're going to show you once and for all what a joke you punks really are. Then maybe you'll leave on your own."

"We're going to hurt you bad," promised Cole. He slammed his fist into his palm.

"You had an unfair advantage," objected Charlie. "You had one of us."

They looked at Banks. "Take him back," offered Rick. "He didn't have the heart of a Warrior anyway."

"C'mon, Adam," Charlie told him. "You're with us now." Adam rejoined his friends. Rick and his crew turned to leave.

"Hey, Biff!" Russ called out to Rick. "After we beat you? One more thing." Rick turned, and Russ pointed to the Warrior flagpole. "The Warriors die and the Ducks fly."

27

The next morning at dawn Coach Orion walked up the arena ramp hauling a large rubber barrel. It was still dark, but early-morning light streamed through the windows of the arena and spilled golden rectangles on the ice.

Coach Orion could hardly believe what he saw.

The Ducks—led by Charlie—were already on the ice doing their warm-up laps. He smiled appreciatively as he watched them circle the rink.

Charlie peeled away from the line to meet Coach Orion at center ice. "We're ready," he said. "Coach."

Orion did a quick double take, but Charlie was smiling. There was no hint of sarcasm—just respect.

"Okay, Charlie," Orion said. "Bring in your team."

The team huddled around Coach Orion. He drew their attention up to where the varsity Warrior state championship banners hung in the rafters. They gazed at the banners in silent appreciation.

"I've been doing my homework on the varsity all season," explained Orion. "I'm not going to lie to you. They're good. The way they wiped your faces in the dirt last time was no fluke."

The team groaned in unison at the humiliating reminder. Orion challenged them. "So if you want your pride back, you'd better be willing to work. There's nothing glamorous about it. In the pros, we call it blue-collar hockey."

The Ducks paid close attention as Coach Orion pulled an empty tuna fish can from the barrel. He dropped it onto the ice.

"There's one thing the varsity does very well," he continued as he next pulled a stale bagel from the barrel and dropped it, too, onto the ice. The kids looked at each other curiously.

"They're vultures around the net." He held up an old soda can. "They find every piece of loose trash. That's how they beat you. Not with the first shot, but the second . . . and the third. They bang in the junk. If we're going to win, we have to pick up the garbage." He lifted up the barrel and dumped its contents onto the ice.

He waited. "So?" he asked. "What do you all say?"

The kids began grunting enthusiastically.

"Let's do it!" shouted Fulton. They all picked up the chant.

The freshman team formed two lines on either side of the net and began to slap pieces of garbage at Julie.

Connie controlled an empty soda can. Guy jostled for an old bottle of shoe polish. Ken rebounded an apple core. Luis a rubber toy.

After about twenty minutes of furious drilling, Orion blew shrilly on his whistle. He angrily called them into a huddle around a box.

"You kids aren't skating like Warriors!" he ranted.

What the? . . .

"No, sir!" he thundered. "You look like something else. You look like . . . Ducks."

Huh?????

He reached into the box and pulled out their old Ducks game jerseys. The kids couldn't believe it.

Orion shrugged. "What?" he asked innocently. He handed out all the jerseys and the kids eagerly slipped them on.

"Okay," Orion said at last. "Who knows what Ducks do best?"

Charlie beamed. *"Fly!"*

28

The arena was standing room only. The mood of the crowd was electric. When the junior varsity team skated out onto the ice, the freshman fans and supporters burst into a huge ovation.

The Ducks circled to center ice.

"For Hans," said Charlie. The players uncoiled from the huddle and made a turn on the ice. One player after another took off a glove and touched the ice.

From the radio booth, the student announcer explained to the crowd the significance of the gesture. *"It looks like the junior varsity team is paying homage to their departed friend and mentor, Hans. Touching the ice is a Norwegian sign of respect."*

There was no sign of respect, however, from

the varsity team as it lumbered onto the ice and began its warm-ups.

At the horn, both coaches pulled their teams over for last-minute instructions.

"They don't belong on the ice with us!" Coach Wilson barked to his players. "Now get out there and PROVE IT!"

On the other side of the ice, Coach Orion tried to calm down his players. "Let's go hunting for goose eggs!" He stuck his hand out. "All right! On three. Quack! Quack! Quack!"

That did it. The tension was shattered immediately. The players picked up the chant as they skated onto the ice. Soon the entire building was thundering with the booming chant of "Quack! Quack! Quack!"

On the opening face-off, Adam slid the puck back to Charlie on defense. Charlie waited for Cole to barrel down on him, then flicked the puck sideways to Fulton, who kicked it into the attacking zone.

A varsity defender stole the puck and passed it to Rick. He immediately charged across the blue line into the neutral zone. At center ice he was hipchecked by Adam Banks. The puck changed hands and was shot back into the varsity zone.

"You're going to wish like hell you stayed with us," snarled Rick after the hard check.

"Save the trash talk," snapped Adam.

Cole controlled the puck and flew up the left wing. Fulton knocked him hard into the boards. The crowd cringed at the impact. In the scramble for the puck, Rick came away with it and immediately tried to deke Connie.

But Connie shook the fake and squirted the puck free. She kicked it up to Fulton on the wing.

A minute had elapsed in regulation. On the bench, Coach Orion gave his team a thumbs-up. They were playing smart, hard hockey.

After an offside call, Julie whipped off her mask. She was breathing hard. She took a huge swig of water as Charlie skated up and tapped her lightly on the shin pad.

"Way to hang tough," he told her.

Adam skated up to Charlie. "These guys keep charging. What are we going to do?"

Charlie was pumped. He was a man on a mission.

"We're going to stand up to them," he told Adam. "And play a little DEFENSE!"

Later in the period, the varsity center broke the blue line and slid a pass to his left wing. He made a quick slap shot. Goldberg decided to play a little defense. Standing about ten feet out in front of the net, Goldberg suddenly dropped and took the puck on the hip. The puck dropped to the ice and Goldberg leaped on it before a varsity player could dig it out.

"Thanks, Goldberg," Julie called out.

Goldberg bowed nonchalantly. "Nothing but garbage."

The period ended with no score.

Rick slammed his helmet onto the bench. Coach Wilson fumed at his players.

"Pick up the hitting! You're playing like a bunch of old ladies out there!" He warned his players, "Now get out there and HIT THEM!"

On the first offensive scrimmage, the varsity pushed the puck deep into the freshman zone. Guy circled behind the net. But when he tried to clear the puck, he was clotheslined with a ferocious forearm. He crashed hard to the ice.

Orion called time-out and helped escort Guy off the ice.

From the bench Coach Wilson clapped and gave his team the fist salute. Orion glared at him from across the ice, but Wilson shrugged.

On another play Adam was maneuvering the puck up the right wing across the blue line when three players converged on him. A hard body block stopped him cold. He took a sharp blow to the ribs and an elbow to the face. His head snapped back so hard his helmet sailed off into the stands.

On the bench Orion was irate. He jumped up and screamed at the referee.

"Hey, Ref! That's not a necklace you're wearing! Blow the stupid thing!"

Connie and Guy helped Adam to the bench.

"I'm okay," he said woozily. He begged Orion not to take him out.

"Son," Orion said, "you're hurt."

Adam pushed himself defiantly to his feet. "I said I'm okay. Put me back in."

Orion nodded slowly. "Okay."

Coach Orion paced the sidelines nervously. He looked up at the clock. Only a few minutes left in the second period. He wondered how much more punishment his players could take before they broke.

"Watch out, Ducks!" he called out. "They're head-hunting!"

Rick made a breakaway move and Fulton and Goldberg double-teamed him. But Rick threw up his elbows at the last second and caught Goldberg square on the chin. Again he went down.

The crowd winced. Orion slammed his palms against the glass in frustration. Averman was next to go down. Then Ken was bodychecked low.

The seconds ticked off the clock. Orion sighed impatiently as he watched his team take a pounding.

With just a few seconds to go, Julie made a dazzling save of what looked like a sure goal. The Ducks controlled the puck and zoomed down the ice in a breakaway. Charlie slipped through a maze of defenders and took the puck on a flip pass in the slot.

Two seconds to go.

He set up for a slap shot. One second . . .

The horn sounded ending the second period.

Charlie pulled up and threw up his hands in frustration. Cole roared up from behind him and threw a blind-side forearm to the back of Charlie's head.

The two benches emptied and a brawl broke out on the ice.

"This isn't hockey!" the radio announcer declared breathlessly. "It's war! The two teams are really going at it. It's a bench clearer, folks. Well, the refs have just stepped in to restore order. The two teams have headed off to the locker rooms. Two periods down and no score. I don't know. You've got to wonder how long this freshman team can take this pounding. It's been brutal!"

The freshman locker room resembled an emergency ward. They were bruised and battered and beaten. Guy was sitting on the bench. His shirt was off and his shoulder had been splinted and taped. Fulton was having his badly swollen ankle retaped.

Charlie had an ice pack to the back of his head.

Averman was limping aimlessly around the locker room. "I feel like my back was being used for trampoline practice."

"Better your back than your face," muttered Adam. He already had the makings of a nasty shiner under one eye and a badly bruised jaw.

Their morale was dropping faster than a thermometer in the Arctic. Orion decided they needed to adjust the game plan.

"That was completely out of line," he told them. "We can't win by fighting them."

"We can't win by shooting, either," Russ observed. "We only got two shots on goal in two periods."

Coach Orion tried to get them to look on the bright side.

"They're getting tired, too. You're playing hard. I'm proud of you."

"They're cheap-shotting us to death," said Luis.

"I know." Orion realized he was losing them. They were beaten. He knew. And they knew it.

Averman sat down finally and hung his head in his hands.

"It's going to take a miracle for us to hold on."

Just then a miracle walked through the door.

The kids looked up.

No way! Dean Portman marched in casually and unfolded an official-looking piece of paper. He cleared his throat dramatically and read: "Dean Portman is awarded a full athletic and academic scholarship to the Eden Hall Academy." He fluttered the paper. "I had this lying around the house in Chicago. My attorney thought maybe I should sign it. I agreed."

"Attorney?" wondered Charlie. Then he grinned. Of course! *Bombay.*

Portman pulled out a pen, grabbed Ken Wu, and used him as a table as he hastily scrawled his signature.

"Well, boys, it's official. I'm back."

Fulton jumped to his feet and raised both fists into the air. "Viva la Bash Brothers!"

He and Portman cracked high fives.

"All right!" Portman declared. "LET'S GO DANCE ON THEIR SKULLS!"

29

The varsity skated onto the ice supremely confident. They had badly crippled the freshman team. Now it was simply a matter of closing in for the kill.

Above the ice in the pavilion box Tom Riley was ecstatic. There was no way the freshman team would survive another period.

Then he saw something on the ice that gave him pause. He angrily descended to Dean Buckley's side. "Who is that?" he demanded. "He can't play!"

Dean Buckley slid a piece of paper out of his pocket. He handed it to Riley.

"The kid's got a contract, Tom. My hands are tied."

Cole skated by Portman. "Ohhhh," he mooned. "The other Bash Brother. I'm really shaking now."

114

"So you're the big enforcer?" Portman greeted him. "It's a real pleasure meeting you." A big smile. Cole moved his mouth like a fish. He had no idea what to say.

"We've got something in common," Portman continued. "I'm the—"

"Shut up and let's play hockey," barked Cole.

Another big smile. "Whatever you say, Sunshine."

On the first play of the third period Cole went head-to-head with Portman. He flew up the ice like a Sherman tank. But Portman calmly dropped a shoulder just as Cole crashed into him. Cole was lifted clear off the ice. He smashed against the glass, which shattered as if in an explosion.

The Ducks erupted in cheers. The varsity was stunned. Cole stumbled to his feet, shedding shards of glass. He teetered woozily and fell.

Fulton skated up. "Now that's what I call clearing the garbage!"

Portman grinned. "We're just getting warmed up."

Portman, Fulton, and Goldberg performed the Bash Brothers. The crowd went wild.

"Okay," said Portman. "Let's take out some more trash."

The game seesawed back and forth. Every time a Warrior player delivered a hit, a Duck player responded. More important, the Ducks were playing aggressive two-way hockey. Adhesive on defense. Attacking on offense.

With little more than two minutes to play, the game was still scoreless.

Coach Wilson prowled the varsity bench like a man obsessed. The varsity team appeared fatigued. With each second that ticked off the clock, their look of panic increased.

For the varsity a tie would be almost as bad as a loss.

On an attacking five-on-four, Rick crossed into the freshman zone just as Portman probed at the puck with his stick.

Rick sprawled onto the ice like a ton of bricks. *Bleeeeeeeee!!!!!!!!*

Portman was dumbfounded when the referee whistled him for a tripping penalty! Rick scampered to his feet and grinned as Portman skated to the penalty box.

"So long . . . sucker," Rick called out.

"You took a dive!" shouted Portman. "You want to see a real penalty? I'll show you a real penalty." He lunged for Rick, but Charlie quickly skated over and broke them up.

Portman glared after him as he skated to the penalty box.

"Don't let down, Charlie. These guys ain't that tough." He and Charlie high-fived.

"We're going to try, man."

But a few short minutes later disaster struck. On a routine line change, the referee whistled the Ducks for putting too many players on the ice.

Orion tried to remain calm. "Luis, back on the bench. Wu, go to the box." He signaled to the referee. "Time-out!"

The Ducks gathered around Orion. He looked up at the clock.

"The pressure's on them. All we've got to do is hold our ground. Conway, Banks, and Goldberg . . . we're going with you."

Goldberg hesitated. "Me, Coach?"

Orion nodded. "You, Goldberg. You earned your spot out there. Okay, Ducks, here we go!"

As the Ducks returned to the ice, the chant of "Defense" built up in a slow tom-tom beat until it reverberated through the arena like a booming kettle drum.

Orion pulled Charlie aside. "Charlie, we're really backed up into a corner here. We're outnumbered, outmuscled, and even a tie seems impossible."

Charlie stiffened with resolve. "We're up to it."

"I know you are." He gave Charlie a small smile. "But you deserve to win." Charlie brightened. Orion nodded. "That's right. Not careless, but not too careful. You see the chance, you take it . . . and make it count."

"Oh, and one more thing." Orion reached behind him. He picked up a felt *C* and placed it over Charlie's heart.

"Go get 'em, Captain."

30

The puck dropped. There was a fierce slashing of sticks. The puck squirted free, and Rick hustled it down. He flipped it back to the point. The varsity probed the defense with a series of passes back and forth.

Suddenly the puck was whipped behind the net. Rick tried to whipsaw it in, but Julie made a great diving save. Still, the puck juddered loose in front of the net. Julie dived for the loose puck . . . and missed!

Adam Banks made a desperate lunge across the crease and batted the puck just wide of the post.

Less than one minute to go.

On a Duck turnover, Rick spiraled out of his zone, caught a flip pass, and initiated a well-timed breakaway that caught the Duck defense off balance. Ahead of the pack, Rick charged across the center line.

Charlie dropped back. Rick threw a fake to his left. But Charlie shrugged it off. Charlie upended him with a perfect hip check. Rick teetered and sprawled on the ice.

Charlie gathered up the loose puck just as Cole charged down on him like a sixteen-wheeler. Charlie had no time to think.

Up in the radio booth the announcer went wild. "I don't believe it! It's the Spinorama! Folks, Conway faked that defender right out of his shorts!"

The crowd leaped to their feet. They began to stamp their feet. The arena trembled from the pounding of the ovation.

It was his dream, Charlie thought. The moment. Only this wasn't a dream. It was really happening.

Charlie had only the goalie to beat.

He held on to the last second. The goalie dropped into his crouch. Charlie jerked back his arm. The goalie lunged forward and dropped. But instead of shooting, at the last possible second Charlie whipped the puck behind and around him. It was a spectacular pass that completely bewildered the goalie.

At the point, Gary Goldberg was amazed to see

the puck coming toward him.

He froze.

On the bench the players screamed, "SHOOT!"

Goldberg looked down matter-of-factly at the puck.

"SHOOT!"

The goalie frantically climbed to his feet and was leaning to cut down the angle to the net.

"SHOOOOOOOOOOOOOT!"

Goldberg gave the puck a sharp slap and watched it slide just under the goalie's out-stretched glove and into the net.

The last few seconds ticked away. The horn sounded. The game was over.

Junior varsity 1; varsity 0.

There was a stampede as the freshman support-ers streamed out of the stands onto the ice. The freshman players mobbed Goldberg.

"Don't ever do that to me again!" kidded Goldberg ecstatically.

"I knew you could do it!" said Charlie. He thumped him on the back.

Orion came running onto the ice.

"That was one heck of a pass, Captain."

"Thanks, Coach."

The ice was crowded with parents and fans, hugging and cheering.

Charlie found Casey and they hugged.

"I'm proud of you, Charlie."

Buoyed along by the thronging and swaying of the crowd, Charlie looked up into the stands. For a second he thought he saw Gordon Bombay. Then he was gone. Vanished.

High above the ice a homemade sign was unfurled from the rafters. It depicted the Ducks in Warrior colors. The crowd erupted in joyous approval.

Linda huddled up to Charlie. She gave him a big kiss on the cheek.

"Thanks, Charlie."

Charlie followed the rope that led from the rafters down to the corner of the arena. He beamed. It *was* Gordon Bombay. He was smiling at Charlie like a proud father.

Charlie fought his way through the cheering crowd to the entrance to the tunnel. Gordon stopped and turned to look at Charlie over his shoulder. He nodded.

Good-bye, Charlie.

He continued walking . . . and was gone.

Charlie smiled. He turned and saw Coach Orion being hoisted onto the shoulders of his teammates. He threw himself into the crowd.

Charlie was lost in its embrace. And happy.